# A NOVEL WAY TO DIE

A Bookish Cafe Mystery Book 6

HARPER LIN

A Novel Way to Die

www.harperlin.com

ISBN: 978-1-987859-96-6

# Chapter 1

It was the sound of champagne bottles popping, or maybe it was the small band playing bossa nova, or maybe it was all the talking and laughing that was the problem. All Maggie Bell knew was that her landlady, Mrs. Peacock, had parties that were talked about for weeks after the fact and this one was going to be no exception. Not that Maggie would know why they were so fabulous, since she wasn't invited.

"You have to understand, dear, this is for a rather boring group of people," Mrs. Peacock said to Maggie three days before the event. "Why, I don't think any of them crack a smile all year until they come to my house."

"Yes, ma'am." Maggie nodded as she stood on the front stoop of the quaint cottage she rented on Mrs. Peacock's property.

"I've had to tighten my belt and limit my guest list already. Normally, I have eight crates of champagne, and this year there will only be five. I just can't afford any more than that. I'm on a fixed income. Money doesn't grow on trees," she huffed as she folded her bejeweled fingers in front of her. Everyone in town knew Mrs. Peacock was a wealthy widow. But to hear her talk, she was just days away from standing in line for government cheese.

"No, ma'am," Maggie replied.

"So, you'll understand when I tell you that it wouldn't be proper to have my tenant roaming the grounds and through my home as the party is going on. Perhaps you've got a friend you can stay with, or maybe you'd like to check into a hotel for the night. I just wouldn't want the noise to keep you up when I know you have to work." Mrs. Peacock smiled as if there was nothing wrong at all with her request.

"Um, well, I don't have to do that," Maggie muttered. "I'll just stay in the house. I'm really not all that interested in parties, and I—"

"Oh, dear. Stay in your house? Oh, that just won't do. I want people to be able to roam the grounds. You have seen how beautifully the garden has come along this year. I must admit it might be the most beautiful in all of Fair Haven. Mrs. Donovan is going to have to pose naked in her yard if she'll want to beat me in the garden walk this year." She rocked on her toes and looked at Maggie for a moment, waiting for her to concur.

"Yes, ma'am" was all Maggie could think to say. She was too busy trying to figure out why she had to leave her home for Mrs. Peacock to have a party. It wasn't like the cottage was even that close to the main house. At least half an acre of blooming lavender, tiger lilies, rose bushes, and a dozen other colorful flowers separated the two domiciles. It wasn't like Maggie made a habit out of visiting Mrs. Peacock in her home. For the past several years that she had been Mrs. Peacock's tenant she'd only been in the house a total of four times.

"So, you'll make other arrangements for Friday night. Wonderful." Mrs. Peacock smiled broadly and blinked pleasantly. "That will be for the best."

Maggie wrinkled her nose, swiveled around, and looked behind her in case there was someone there who'd agreed to this request on her behalf. But there wasn't. She was all alone and hadn't flinched. But somehow Mrs. Peacock took that as an affirmative to her request.

"I don't think I can…" Maggie started, but Mrs. Peacock was already walking back to the house, mumbling to herself. She stopped to pick at a stalk of lavender, then, deciding it wasn't worth any more attention, hurried back to the main house. Over the next three days, Maggie watched Mrs. Peacock order around a party planner who had lighting strung, speakers placed, and a temporary lounge set up in her yard. It looked beautiful.

As the sun started to set on Friday night, the guests started to arrive. It was as if nature itself wanted to make Mrs. Peacock's party a smashing success. The sky was mostly clear as it turned orange, pink, and purple with a few stratus clouds that were a rich periwinkle just above the horizon.

The white lights strung from the trees and through the pathway in the garden popped on. The band started to play inside as the speakers brought the jazzy sound outdoors. It didn't take long for handsome couples to start roaming the grounds carrying glasses of champagne.

Little did Mrs. Peacock know that her tenant, Maggie Bell, had planned a little party of her own. An exclusive guest list that consisted of herself and no one else. Chinese takeout that she'd picked up especially for this occasion was waiting in the fridge. Four strategically placed candles that would provide her with just enough light to get her from the front room to the kitchen, the bathroom, and her bedroom without having to feel her way along the walls.

The cottage looked like no one was home. But Maggie was there watching from her front room window, in the dark.

"This is the best party I've ever been to," she muttered to herself after getting her Chinese food on a plate and taking a seat in her comfy high-backed chair that she'd picked up at a thrift store a while back. She sat directly in front of her window, but no one could see her through the Irish lace curtains. The breeze that blew was soft and cool. Everything was rather wonderful, Maggie thought, as she munched an eggroll before digging into her pepper steak and rice. But just as she took a sip of her iced tea, she froze.

"What's that place?" A quartet of partygoers

had found their way along the path to Maggie's cottage. Two men and two women.

*This is not good,* Maggie thought.

"It's a little house. Isn't that adorable. It's like a maid's quarters or something like in *Downton Abbey,*" one of the women said.

Maggie wrinkled her nose and pinched her eyebrows. *Maid's quarters? Downton Abbey?*

"Let's go look inside," the other man said.

What was wrong with these people? This was private property. They were at a party. *Why don't you go snoop in Mrs. Peacock's place? She's got much nicer things,* Maggie thought as she set her jaw and slipped off her chair and away from the window.

"No. If Vivian allowed us to go in there, she'd have told us. There would be lights on, that's for sure. I'll break my neck in these heels if I try and walk on that soggy ground," the other woman said.

*Finally, a grown-up. Of course she's the voice of reason. She's the only one in modest dress,* Maggie thought. *Wait. Soggy ground? What soggy ground?*

"I'm going to see if it's unlocked," the first man said.

Maggie hoped the ground *was* soggy and that he sunk his fancy shoes deep in it up to the cuffs of his pants.

"Matt, stop. This isn't your property," the classy woman in the simple black dress said, trying to pull her date's hand. He pulled away and came up my walk. I couldn't believe the nerve as he peeked around the front door, took hold of the knob, and tried to jiggle it open.

"It's locked. I wonder if I could break a window without anyone noticing," Matt said as he looked over his shoulder.

"Matthew Spencersmith, you better not do anything of the sort," the only classy woman in this quartet said.

"Come on, Mona. Don't be such a dud," Matt replied.

"Yeah, Mona. I thought you liked to be adventurous," the other woman, who thought she was a font of knowledge regarding maid's quarters, piped up. Her dress was short, and her heels were high, but that didn't stop her from sidling up to Matt at the front door. It seemed her own date had no opinion on the matter at all and said nothing.

"Trespassing isn't adventurous, Colleen," Mona snapped back. They didn't exactly sound like friends.

*Matthew Spencersmith? Where have I heard that name?* Maggie mused. But the sound of her jiggling doorknob and the threat of a rock coming through her window made her push that out of her mind, and she did something she'd never done before. She braced herself for a confrontation. On tiptoes, she stepped to her door and was just about to yank it open to scold them outright when they were saved by someone at the house calling Matthew.

"Come on. They're looking for you. And we're missing the party," Mona said.

"All right. We'll go back," Matthew said and stepped up to his date to give her what Maggie thought was a patronizing kiss on the cheek.

"Aww. Party pooper," Colleen huffed and finally went back to the man who was her date. He still said nothing as Matthew took Mona's hand and pulled her toward the house, taking long strides to her tiny, heel-impaired steps.

That was enough to make Maggie decide right then and there that she was getting motion lights put on her cottage. The receipt would be going to Mrs. Peacock. What kind of people was she inviting to her house? Now, instead of sitting back and listening to the music and chatter as a voyeur, Maggie felt she was sitting up to guard her residence from the drunk and disorderly.

The party went on for a couple of hours. Just

when Maggie thought things were winding down and the sound of good-byes and car doors slamming shut could be heard, she saw someone making their way to her cottage down the path from the main house. She squinted and pouted her lips as she watched him through the curtains. It was Matthew Spencersmith. He walked up to the cottage and looked over his shoulder, and that was when Maggie heard the most alarming sound and could remain hidden no more. It was the sound of a zipper.

"Hey! There are bathrooms in the main house!" she shouted.

"What? Who?" Matthew Spencersmith quickly zipped up and staggered back a couple of steps before leaning on his knees to peer at the house.

"I'm going to tell Mrs. Peacock what you were about to do if you don't get away from my house." Maggie was surprised at how brave she was in the dark house with a stranger outside.

"I'm sorry. I'm sorry," he slurred. "Hey. Who's in there?"

"Mrs. Peacock's tenant. She's going to hear about you and your friends thinking of breaking into the guest house and you using her yard as a public toilet."

"No. No. You don't have to tell her anything.

I'm so sorry. I've had a little too much to drink. You know how it is," the man continued to ramble.

Maggie wrinkled her nose with disgust. "Fine. If you just go away and—"

"You've got a pretty voice. Why don't you come out here and talk to me? Face-to-face," he said. Maggie's stomach flipped as she imagined the sour smell of alcohol and sweat on him, and his suit wrinkled and stained.

"No thanks," she replied.

"I won't bite. I promise," he replied with a chuckle.

Maggie heard more car doors slamming shut and engines starting. "Your date is going to leave without you. You better get going."

"She's not going anywhere without me. Do you know who I am? I'm Matthew Spencersmith. The youngest and most eligible city councilman Fair Haven has ever elected, with a very bright political future," he boasted. Maggie thought he sounded like he'd said that to his reflection in the mirror a thousand times before tonight.

"Well, Mr. Spencersmith, I think you better find her and maybe a cup of black coffee," Maggie chirped from the darkness of her home. She felt a little bit like Cyrano de Bergerac, who was able to be honest and brave with Roxanne while he was in the shadows. Had she been in front of Mr. Spencersmith, she would have probably stood there awkwardly, her face twisted in discomfort and not a single word to say popping into her head.

"Black coffee. That's funny. Very funny. Hey, can I come in and use your bathroom?" he asked in all seriousness.

"No. Absolutely not," Maggie replied.

"It's kind of an emergency," he continued.

"Then you better hurry back to the main house," Maggie urged him.

Matthew Spencersmith turned and started to lurch his way back to the house. There were still some partygoers there. But the music had stopped, and from what Maggie could see in the soft patio lights, the cleaning crew had started to break things down and quietly put the yard back in order.

Finally, after none of the remaining guests seemed too interested in walking Mrs. Peacock's grounds at such a late hour, Maggie decided it was safe to go to bed. When she woke up to her alarm, she felt tired and cranky. When she looked in the mirror before leaving her house for the bookstore, she was sure everyone was going to know she had a rough night and ask her a lot of questions. But

Maggie never made it to work. As soon as she had stepped out her front door and taken three steps toward her car, she stopped.

There, lying on the ground with a severe blow to his head, was Matthew Spencersmith. He was dead.

## Chapter 2

As if the crowd from the previous night and the lack of sleep wasn't enough to set her on edge, Maggie felt her chest tighten as Officer Gary Brookes pulled up in his squad car along with an ambulance, the coroner, the crime scene photographer, and a couple of other officers there for crowd control and to tape off the perimeter of Maggie's cottage.

"Maggie? Are you all right?" Gary asked softly as he approached. She was sitting on the stoop with her hands in her lap and her hair wild and kinked from the mist in the air.

He was a big guy with a barrel chest even without his bulletproof vest. She looked at the tattoos on his meaty arms as he approached but let out a breath of relief and shrugged when she saw his kind face. Gary had a way of making her feel a little more comfortable in her skin. Probably because they'd known each other through the most awkward period of a young person's life: high school.

Without hesitating, he took a seat next to her, pulled out his pocket notebook and a pencil, and asked her to start at the beginning.

"I wasn't supposed to be here," she confided. "Mrs. Peacock didn't want me anywhere near the party. She suggested I stay at a hotel. I don't have the money to stay at a hotel at a moment's notice. So I hid out in my own house."

"Have you talked to Vivian yet?" he asked, knowing the answer before Maggie spat out the word no.

"I figured I'd wait until you could be here to throw yourself in front of her. You know. Just in case the claws come out," Maggie huffed and wrinkled her nose as she made clawing gestures with her hands.

"How long have you lived here? You know Vivian Peacock is the world's biggest softy on her fixed income." Gary smirked. "She's not going to be angry that you stayed in the house you are paying rent to live in."

Maggie nodded.

"Hey. What have you got going on over there?" Gary asked, pointing to a freshly dug patch of earth and some lawn tools in a box propped up at the corner of the house.

Maggie took a deep breath. "I planted some sunflowers and some of those black-eyed Susans. I thought they'd look nice along the side of the house and maybe camouflage it a little. I don't know if they'll grow. I followed the instructions."

"That's great. I'm a bit of an amateur gardener myself. I find it relaxing," Gary said as he stood up, letting out a slight grunt. Maggie smiled. He was such a tough-looking guy that the idea of him in Crocs talking to some tomato plants and urging them to grow went against the grain. But, like Vivian Peacock, he was also one of those big softies.

"What is going on here?" came the shrill screech of Mrs. Peacock. "What are the police doing on my property? Excuse me! Excuse me? Officer... oh, yes. Officer Brookes. What's going on here? What has happened?"

Gary wasted no time and without a parting word

to Maggie walked over to Mrs. Peacock to break the news that one of her partygoers was found dead on her property. Maggie watched as the eccentric old lady's hand went to her lips and her eyes went wide. She looked up at Gary as he softly spoke and pointed to Maggie. All at once it was like someone had pulled the outer corners of Mrs. Peacock's eyes down as she slowly approached Maggie.

"I thought you were staying at a hotel?" she asked.

"I really couldn't afford it, Mrs. Peacock. I just hid out with the lights off and had a nice time until I was afraid Mr. Spencersmith was going to break in. I'm sorry," Maggie replied.

Mrs. Peacock shook her head. She whispered something to Gary, but he only chuckled and shook his head. Maggie was sure it was something about her and probably negative. But still she kept quiet.

"What is that?" Mrs. Peacock pointed to the paramedics and the crime scene photographer snapping away photo after photo.

"That's Mr. Spencersmith," Gary replied.

"Oh no. It's only a matter of time before the press shows up." Mrs. Peacock put her hand on Gary's arm but looked dramatically from her house to the crime scene and back to her home. Maggie was sure she was trying to figure out how to get to her phone and call her favorite nemesis, Mrs. Donovan, who lived a couple of blocks away, and spill as many gory details as possible in a five-minute phone conversation.

"I'm sorry, Vivian. But the man involved was a politician," Gary said. "I'll do my best, but due to the nature of this situation, I don't think I'll be able to keep this one quiet."

"What?" Maggie snapped as she stood up. "What do you mean?"

Gary shrugged. "Sorry, Mags. But the press is gonna run with this one. You know it. So there might be some people wanting to ask you some questions. But you don't have to answer them. In fact, I'd suggest you don't."

In her head, Maggie had a thousand reasons why the police and Mrs. Peacock should sit on this situation. Nervously, she looked at all the emergency vehicles on the street and to her horror already saw some rubberneckers. The news was spreading as she was sitting there.

"Do you know how he died?" Mrs. Peacock asked.

"From what I could see, it looked like he was clunked on the head pretty good. But we won't know for sure until the coroner has a look at him."

"Could he have hit his head falling down? He had a good bit to drink last night," Mrs. Peacock admitted.

"We won't know anything until the autopsy is finished. But I suppose that's a possibility," Gary replied without making any kind of commitment.

"Do you think it could be something else?" Maggie asked.

"At this point, Mags, it could be anything. We just have to wait," he replied. Maggie wasn't sure what he meant, but she didn't like the vagueness that seemed to be floating around every answer he gave. Were they thinking this could have been foul play? That would get the spotlight on her for sure. This day couldn't have started any worse.

"Officer Brookes, would you like to come inside for a cup of coffee or water?" Mrs. Peacock asked as she nervously rubbed her hands together.

"No, ma'am. I'm going to have to stay out here until they are done." He pointed to the crew collecting evidence along with the body.

"What about me, Gary? Do I need to stick around?" Maggie asked as she shifted from her right leg to her left.

"If I have any more questions, I know where to find you." Gary grinned. She couldn't help but notice how handsome he looked. It made her squint and twist her lips as she pulled her keys from her pocket and headed toward her car. Mrs. Peacock let Gary know she'd be in the house, calling her dear friend, Mrs. Donovan, in the hopes she could come by and keep her company through this horrific experience.

Maggie could imagine that conversation. *Hello, Mrs. Donovan. Sorry you couldn't come to my party last night since you weren't invited because* you *didn't invite* me *to your last party. But I've got the police here because Matthew Spencersmith is dead in my yard. Good luck topping that!*

But then something even worse than finding a dead body near her house first thing in the morning happened. A reporter with a camera saw Maggie getting in her Dodge Neon and snapped a picture.

"Oh drat!" she shouted inside the car with the windows rolled up. Mrs. Peacock would have loved for the press to take her picture. She always photographed well, she said. If she couldn't get written up over the success of her party, she didn't mind getting written up in a scandal that occurred during or after her party. But that was one of the millions of things that separated Mrs. Peacock from Maggie. The last thing Maggie wanted was attention. She hurried to the bookstore, parked her car, and took a deep breath. She felt like everyone walking on the sidewalk or driving by was looking at her.

"It's just your imagination, Mags. Get ahold of yourself. The body's probably not even cold. The news hasn't even taken hold anywhere yet." She tried to soothe herself as she got out of the car and scurried to the door, her keys in her hand.

She managed to slip inside and lock the door behind her to savor a few minutes before opening for business. The smell of fresh-brewed coffee was comforting. Babs, the voluptuous blonde who looked like she'd stepped out of an episode of *Happy Days,* ran the coffee shop and had already gotten things baking and brewing. Maggie shuffled into the café and up to the counter.

"Hey, Mags. Whoa, you look like you tied one on last night. Don't tell me you crashed Old Lady Peacock's shindig and now have a case of the booze flu," Babs said in one breath.

"No. But I feel like I have a hangover. Can I get a coffee? Black, please," Maggie asked.

"Sure. On the house," Babs said and gave her a

large cup to fill from the carafe on the bar ledge to the left. "Are you all right?"

Maggie looked over her shoulder. "A guy named Matthew Spencersmith was found dead in my yard this morning. He was a guest at Mrs. Peacock's party."

Babs's whole face turned into one giant O. Her eyes. Her mouth. The shape of her face. Maggie almost started to laugh.

"Matthew Spencersmith is dead? Oh, I have got to call Roy. He and Earl are probably watching *Thomas the Tank Engine* about now," she said before picking up the phone from the back of the café, where the ovens and baking supplies were. The phone had a cord that stretched almost twenty feet.

"Can you wait? I mean, the police are at the house. A reporter took my picture as I was leaving. I just want to put off any attention as long as possible," she grumbled as she pumped the lever to get her coffee.

"Oh. Of course, honey. Actually, Roy likes *Thomas* more than the baby does. I probably shouldn't interrupt," Babs said and put the phone back. "Do they know what happened?"

"He was clunked on the back of the head.

That's all I know. Babs, can I tell you something without you thinking I'm a horrible person?"

"I'd never think that of you, Mags." She smiled and winked one of her black-lined, false-eyelashed eyes.

Maggie explained Matthew Spencersmith's behavior when he and the group of people stumbled upon her cottage. She also mentioned him wanting to come in and use her bathroom.

"I thought he was a complete jerk. You shouldn't be killed for being a jerk, but I can see where someone wouldn't like him. He was full of himself. Plus… oh, never mind."

"What?"

"I got a really bad vibe from him. Like he was hiding something more than just the fact he wanted to pee outside. I don't know. Maybe I'm just imagining things now cause I'm annoyed." Maggie let out a sigh.

"Oh, that doesn't surprise me," Babs said. "His family is loaded. They act like the Kennedys of Fair Haven. Whatever *that* can get a person. He's got a lot of rumors around him and not all of them good."

"Well, Mona was his date, but I thought that Colleen woman was acting a little too familiar with him. Especially when he suggested breaking into my house. Who does that?" Maggie said before taking a sip of coffee. It instantly made her feel better. The bitter taste of the hot liquid was like drinking a hug. Babs laughed and promised not to tell her husband Roy until she got home.

Maggie thanked her and took her coffee to the bookstore side of the business and snapped the door open before flipping the welcome sign. Poe, the cat, had paid no attention to Maggie when she came in but now had found his place in a square of sunshine on the ledge in front of the windows next to the register. She stroked his short black fur and felt the vibration of his motor happily running.

"Poe, you've got it made. No one ever bothers you," Maggie said before heading to the storeroom where new books had been delivered the previous day. It was only about fifteen minutes after opening when a woman came bustling around a tall book-case and asked for Margaret Bell.

"Who wants to know?" Maggie asked.

"Mona Plum. Matthew Spencersmith's fiancée."

# Chapter 3

"**I**'m Margaret Bell. What do you want?" Maggie squinted and looked Mona up and down. She was professionally dressed and wore very little jewelry, like she was going on a job interview or had an appointment with a lawyer.

"I understand that you live on Vivian Peacock's property. We were at her event last night, and I don't recall being introduced to you." She stood there, her eyes like those sewn into a stuffed teddy bear. She stared and didn't blink, making Maggie feel uneasy.

After shaking off the annoyance, Maggie took a deep breath and wondered how the news could have spread so fast. Maggie furrowed her eyebrows and tugged at the cuffs of her sleeves, as she often did when uncomfortable.

"I wasn't at the party. I stayed in my house. It's the little cottage off the far end of the property. There is a patch of lavender across the path from it," she said and waited for Mona to recall her fiancé threatening to break in. That fact seemed to evade Mona's memory.

"My fiancé is dead," Mona said.

"Boy, news travels fast," Maggie mumbled, more to herself, but Mona took umbrage.

"You think this is some kind of joke?"

"No. I never said that. I'm just shocked at how quickly word spread. Miss Plum, I'm sorry for your loss. I'm sure the police told you that…"

"Matthew would have never been killed had he not been at your house."

"He wasn't at my house. He stumbled there and wanted to use my bathroom. Well, actually, he was going to use my yard as a bathroom but—"

"Don't you lie to me. I know what kind of man he was, and I accepted him anyway. He loved me. He didn't love you. You were just a toy and—"

Maggie choked on the air. "What? Hey, I never saw him before last night! I believe you and Mr.

Spencersmith and two other people came dangerously close to my house."

Finally, Mona blinked. "You were there all night?"

"Why are you asking? I already talked to the police and told them everything that I knew about last night."

"What exactly did you tell them, Margaret?"

Maggie took a step back and folded her arms around her waist. She didn't feel comfortable talking with Mona. There was a strangeness about the woman that reminded Maggie of the eccentric old lady who murdered her husband in the book *Dolores Claiborne*.

"I'm not sure I like talking about this," Maggie replied.

"Oh, you don't like it?" Mona took a small step forward.

"No."

"I don't like the fact that you were in your house the whole time he slipped away from the party. Did anyone else come to your house last night? Hmm?"

Maggie wrinkled her nose and twisted her mouth. "What are you talking about?"

"What are you going to do? Sell your story to the first tabloid to make you an offer? Make a few dollars on my fiancé's name? Start a scandal when he's not able to defend himself? I know your type, Miss Bell," Mona hissed.

"I'd never seen your fiancé in my life until last night. Before that I think I only heard the name Matthew Spencersmith once or twice in the news," Maggie offered, still with her arms wrapped around herself.

"Do you think I'm stupid?" Mona's voice was quiet but full of venom.

"I don't think you have your facts straight."

"I'm used to Matthew's shenanigans. I knew when the car came around and he wasn't anywhere to be found that I'd be cleaning up his mess again. So I was coming back for him. But for you to think you can horn in on the Spencersmith name and—"

"What's going on here?" Joshua Whitfield suddenly appeared from the front of the store. Maggie was relieved. The cavalry arrived in just the nick of time.

Mona Plum looked Joshua up and down before focusing again on Maggie.

"You'll be hearing from me *and* my lawyer," Mona snapped before turning her back and stomping out of the store. The way she yanked the door open made it tear through the bells, which then jingled furiously.

"What in the world was that all about? I could hear that harpy screeching through the entire store," Joshua said while shaking his head and looking over his shoulder toward the front door. "What did you do, Maggie Bell?"

Maggie stood there for a moment. She wasn't even sure how to answer since she didn't do anything at all to anyone. But as far as Mona Plum was concerned, Margaret Bell should have a scarlet *A* stitched on the front of her clothes.

"I really have no idea," she replied.

# Chapter 4

Joshua Whitfield was Maggie's boss and today looked like an absolute dreamboat wearing a flannel shirt, blue jeans, and a tool belt. Even though he owned The Bookish Café, having inherited it from his father, Alexander Whitfield, Joshua loved the daily maintenance of the place more than anything else. Maggie was thankful for that, as she enjoyed the solitude of dealing with the shipments and organizing the shelves while keeping things neat and orderly. If only she didn't have to deal with customers. The most recent one being no exception.

"What was she saying about Matthew Spencer-smith?" Joshua asked.

"Well, he's dead and——"

"What? He's dead?"

"Yeah. He was in my front yard. It's been over forty-five minutes since he was discovered. How come you don't know about it?" Maggie put her hands on her hips and twisted up her face.

"Uh, maybe because he was just found in your yard? I don't know. Oh my gosh. This is crazy. Maggie, what did you do?" Joshua teased, but Maggie wasn't in the mood.

"Mona Plum seems to think that Matthew and I were having some kind of affair. I never even met the guy. Even if I had, I could tell from last night that I wouldn't have wanted anything to do with the likes of him." Maggie brushed her curls away from her face.

"Why? Did he prefer movies to reading the books?" Joshua continued to tease.

"Ha ha. No, he was no gentleman," Maggie replied and told him of her experience with Matthew, Mona, Colleen, and the silent man who were near her home, as well as Matthew's second visit. She shook her head with disgust.

"That is weird. So, she thinks you were having an affair with her fiancé?" Joshua asked.

"I guess so." Maggie frowned like she'd just tasted something sour. Then she snapped her fingers. "How in the world did she get the news about Matthew's death so quickly? You didn't know."

"Uh, well, maybe…" Joshua shrugged. "I don't know."

"She said she was coming back to my place to collect him and… Oh! Maybe she's the one who clunked him on the head and is trying to cover her tracks. That's the only thing I can think of. I should call Gary and tell him."

"Mags, maybe cool your jets for a little while. First, Matthew Spencersmith is going to stay dead. So there is no hurry. Second, you just had a really bizarre encounter with his distraught and jealous fiancée. Maybe let everything sink in and write down what she said then later today give Gary a call." Joshua's suggestion sounded logical. Maggie bit her thumbnail for a second but then nodded in agreement. She'd do what he said and let the incident marinate for a while before contacting the authorities.

There were books that needed to be put away that she picked up by the armful from the storeroom and wandered the aisles slipping them in their appropriate categories. That was when she found it. A shredded book just lying on the floor.

"What?" she gasped. It was one thing to question her morals or behavior, but it was something completely different to shred a book out of anger. "*Confessions of a Window Dresser?* I wanted to read this book. This is completely unacceptable and... quite frankly... infuriating!"

Maggie was sure that Mona Plum was behind the vandalism and destruction of property. After all she had been in the store when Maggie was in the back. She'd had plenty of time to commit the crime.

"I'm not sure I'd call it a crime," Joshua replied.

"Oh, *I* would," Maggie snapped back, shaking the tattered pages at her boss.

"If she comes back, I want you to come get me right away. I don't want there to be any further confrontations, and I don't want anyone getting hurt," Joshua said as he climbed up on the ledge next to the register that Poe was still lazily occupying.

"I won't get hurt," Maggie huffed.

"I wasn't talking about you. I was talking about her. I'm glad I never let you see me dog-ear a page for a bookmark. Yikes," Joshua said with a smirk.

Maggie started to smile but felt her cheeks get

red. "This really isn't funny," she muttered, trying to cover up the fact she enjoyed his teasing.

"I've never seen you get so mad. Over a book," Joshua continued.

"This is inventory. Do you even know what this book is about?"

"No. But I don't think I need to know what it's about to see that I can't sell it." He was annoying her on purpose.

Maggie put her hands on her hips. "You're a real comedian this morning."

"Hey, it's not a big deal. I've got real things to tend to, like the lightbulbs in the window. Plus, you have the new display to start working on. Any ideas?"

"Maybe?"

"What do you mean 'maybe'?"

Maggie wrinkled her nose. "I mean I'll tell you when I have an idea."

"Oh, so that's how it's going to be."

"It is."

"You do remember that I'm the boss here?"

"How can I possibly forget?" Maggie wrinkled her nose before she quickly hurried off to the storeroom, where she decided that she'd definitely inform Gary of this barbaric act as soon as she saw him. Carefully, she folded up the pages and set it in the large gray garbage can. It was beyond fixing.

"At least it wasn't one of the first editions. Oh, then I'd hunt her down myself. I've never been in a fistfight in my entire life, but I might just throw a couple punches," Maggie muttered as she picked up another stack of books to add to the shelves.

Still, she couldn't understand why Joshua wasn't more upset with someone destroying store property. Sometimes she thought he did things just to annoy her. This was one of those things. If only he didn't look so good while doing it. If he had a hump like Quasimodo's or a nose like Cyrano's, she might be able to keep her wits about her. But he was handsome and handy, and although he read books on the *New York Times* Best Seller list—that thought made Maggie shudder like she'd been offered a plate of raw liver—he was almost perfect.

*A perfect pain in the behind,* her conscience piped up. When she finally calmed down and there was a lull in customers, she took a seat at Alexander Whitfield's old desk and wrote down what Mona had said to her. It was even stranger as she wrote it out. But there was something that didn't seem right about all of it. Of all the people at the party, why did Mona think Maggie was in on something when she wasn't even a guest? It made no sense. Plus, she said she was coming by her house to pick Matthew up—in the morning? She would have seen all the commotion. Then perhaps Gary had already spoken to her. Maggie was ready to call him as soon as she got home. But as it turned out, she didn't have to. He was snooping in her yard.

## Chapter 5

After pulling her car into the narrow gravel spot Mrs. Peacock allowed Maggie to park her car on just off the southern corner of her house, Maggie cut the engine and climbed out.

"You're just the guy I wanted to talk to. But what are you doing here?" she said.

"Uh, well, I need to talk to you," Gary said. Maggie gave him half a grin but realized he wasn't smiling. If she had to guess she'd say he ate something that didn't agree with him.

"What's wrong?" She shook her head and shrugged her shoulders. "Aside from the fact there was a dead guy in my yard?" How could she have forgotten about Matthew Spencersmith? The whole reason she wanted to talk to Gary was because of him and his wacky fiancée who ambushed her at work. The shredded book made her blood boil.

"Yeah. About that. Can we go in the house and sit down?" Gary was serious. Without making any further comments, Maggie looked down at her keys, nodded, and walked to the front door. She opened up and stepped inside, holding the door for Gary. He had to stoop just a little to come in, and he managed to fill the entire front room. Part of it was his bulletproof vest and utility belt. They had to be a hundred extra pounds alone. But he was a big guy, there was no doubt about that.

Maggie closed the door behind him and invited Gary to the kitchen. He took a seat at the kitchen table and folded his hands politely.

"What's going on, Gary? You look like you're going to be sick," Maggie said as she put on a kettle for some tea.

"First, let me just say I have to do this. It's my job, and just because we are friends doesn't mean I can show any favoritism," he said, looking down at his hands.

Maggie took the seat next to him and patted his big, beefy, tattooed arm. "It's okay, Gary," she said softly.

"We found what we think is the murder weapon," he said. "A hammer."

"Wow. Good. That was quick. That ought to make the case move along a lot quicker. Right? Are there any prints on it?" Maggie asked, her eyes wide with interest.

"Yes. Just one set of prints. Maggie, I need you to come with me to the station to run your prints," Gary said, looking like a dog standing in the kitchen in front of a tipped-over garbage can.

"What? You're joking. This is a joke," she said.

"I'm sorry, Maggie. But I have to." Gary's eyes were soft but stern.

"I don't believe this. You think I killed Matthew Spencersmith? How can you think that? We've known each other for years. I'd never—"

"Of course I don't think you killed him. I've got my theories. Especially since it was an anonymous tip that led me to the murder weapon. But there is a procedure, and I have to follow it, if for no other reason than to make sure you don't get pinned for a crime you didn't commit," Gary said.

"Are you going to cuff me?" Maggie gasped.

"Of course not."

"Oh my gosh! Are you going to put me in the pen? With other criminals?"

"Maggie, first, this is Fair Haven. The most hardened female criminals here are drunks and maybe, *maybe*, a shoplifter. Second, we're just taking your prints. They have to be sent to a lab. And *no*. No one is putting you in *the pen*. My gosh, girl. You've been to the police station a thousand times. The holding cells in Mayberry are harsher than ours."

Maggie leaned back in her chair and took a deep breath. It seemed like nothing good had happened since her first encounter with Matthew Spencersmith.

"What is everyone at the bookstore going to say when this gets out?"

"Are you kidding? They are going to say 'Maggie Bell got fingerprinted by the po-po? Don't mess with Maggie.' That's what they are going to say," Gary replied with a smirk.

She knew he was trying to be sweet, and that little twinkle in his eyes made Maggie smile. But inside she was all in knots. "Speaking of 'don't mess with Maggie,'" she said, "I had a strange visitor at the bookstore today." Having almost forgotten about Mona Plum, Maggie told Gary about the encounter, what was said, and the destruction of the book *Confessions of a Window Dresser*.

"That *is* odd," Gary replied. "Who did you say this was?"

"Mona Plum. Matthew's fiancé. She said she came by here to *collect* him from my residence. That was this morning, and she knew he was dead. I thought she'd spoken to you. How else would she know he was dead?" Maggie knew something was not right, and by the look on Gary's face, he did too. But it didn't change the fact that they had to go to the police station and get her fingerprints.

"Let's get this over with. Then I'll swing by Miss Plum's residence and have a little chat," Gary said. Maggie felt a little better as she stood from the table. Being the gentleman that he was, Gary told Maggie she could drive her own car to the station so as not to attract any additional attention.

"I think that might be best," she replied as she pulled her keys from her pocket.

"Just don't try and give me the slip. I'd hate to report you as a flight risk," he said. Maggie smacked his thick shoulder.

"That's assault on a police officer too. Boy, you are a brute."

Maggie had to laugh. When she did, Gary smiled wide as he watched her. Quickly, she looked down at her keys, the smile still on her face as she hurried to her car. Gary walked briskly to his patrol car and within a few seconds was off down the road. Maggie climbed into her Neon, but before she could get out of the driveway, a man with a pad of paper and a camera around his neck knocked on the passenger-side window.

"Excuse me. Can I have a moment of your time?" He flashed a toothy grin that made Maggie wince.

"Where did you come from?" Maggie quickly hit the button to make sure the doors were locked.

"I'm sorry. I didn't mean to frighten you. I was just waiting until you finished talking with Officer Brookes. My name is Oscar Durham. I write for the Fair Haven Bugle. You're going to the police station, are ya?"

"Back away from my car," Maggie ordered.

"I just wanted to talk to you for a second. Why was Matthew Spencersmith in your house?" Oscar asked, never dropping that garish grin.

"He wasn't in my house," Maggie replied. "Step away from my car!"

"Were you and he good friends?"

"I never met him before! Now please get away from my car! I'm trying to back out!" Maggie insisted as she put the car in reverse.

"I just have a couple more questions. How long have you known Matthew? And did you know he was engaged?" Oscar was a jerk and tried to hang on to the door handle as Maggie backed out. But she didn't stop, and his grip wasn't that good. He was nearly dragged to his knees but managed to stay on his feet long enough to regain his balance and shake his fist at Maggie with a look of utter shock on his face.

"What did he think? I wasn't going to drive away?" She sneered at the thought. This was just another thing she was going to have to tell Gary when she got to the police station. Perhaps he'd take care of it. From the looks of him, Oscar Durham didn't seem like he'd been hitting the gym regularly. But Gary Brookes looked like he did. Plus, he had a temper to match. When Gary found out that someone was insinuating that his friend had committed a crime, Oscar better be ready to answer some questions himself.

"Was he waiting in the bushes? That's so creepy," Maggie whined. This was not going to be an easy situation to maneuver. She had a crazy fiancée out to get her. Her fingerprints were at the crime scene, which happened to be her yard, and a Peeping Tom reporter of sorts was skulking around all the while. By the time she got to the police station, Maggie was trembling.

The headquarters for Fair Haven's finest was a cute little white building with flower boxes and a welcome mat. Inside, Maggie smelled the soothing scent of vanilla coming from the dispatcher's desk.

"Hi, Maggie. What brings you here?" Gloria, the dispatcher, asked before moving the burning scented candle to add another stack of papers to her desk.

"I need to be fingerprinted," Maggie muttered while tugging at her sleeve cuffs.

"You... what?" Gloria was one of those common-sense older women who if she didn't say it out loud was always thinking *Well, bless your heart* around the majority of people that came into the station.

"You heard her right." Gary chuckled. "We've got to rule her out as a suspect. Follow me, young lady. And don't try anything funny."

Maggie pinched her lips and wrinkled her nose. She didn't feel like joking around. In the corner of the office just a little out of arm's reach from the holding cell was the fingerprinting station. It was nothing more than a stack of blank cards, a solid brick of ink, and a couple of pens in a baseball-shaped coffee mug.

"Gary, I need to tell you something," Maggie said as she walked up next to her friend. He dwarfed her, but at the moment she was thankful to be close to him. He would be intimidating to anyone, especially some punk reporter who was stalking her. Maggie told him what happened right after he drove off. He took a deep breath as he tenderly took hold of her thumb on her right hand and rolled it across the ink and then on the pre-printed fingerprint card.

"I told you there were going to be reporters looking into this. I'm sorry. I should have waited for you to get in your car. I won't make that same mistake twice," he muttered as he took her next finger.

"But are they allowed to come on my property or that close to my house? What about work? Oh, this is awful. This Spencersmith guy is really causing me a lot of problems and he's dead. What kind of treachery did he drag around behind him when he was alive?" Maggie huffed.

"Look, just don't say anything to anyone about this," Gary said.

"He knew I was meeting you here at the station." Maggie winced at her own words.

"Yeah, well, he doesn't know what for. We'll make sure we get all this ink off your hands. He can think you were filing a restraining order on him or that you were talking to the biggest, baddest officer on the force who heard he needs to be taught some manners." Gary puffed out his chest. Maggie couldn't help but smile awkwardly.

Finally, he finished and sealed the prints up in a tamper-proof clear baggie to be put in an envelope and sent to forensics in Odell County for comparison.

"Would you let me know when you get the results back?" Maggie finished scrubbing her hands, but the black ink remained around her cuticles.

"Yeah. And I'll walk you to your car this time," he insisted. She said good-bye to Gloria and once outside felt anxious as she scanned the area for signs of the press. It was pretty quiet.

As Gary was talking, Maggie began to feel the realization of what was going on start to seep into her bones. She blurted out the words before she even had a chance to consider such a ludicrous idea.

"Is someone trying to frame me? It sure does feel that way," she yipped.

"Why would anyone want to frame you?" Gary asked as they approached the driver's side of her car.

"I don't know. But this is just too crazy. A guy who I didn't know ends up dead on my property and his fiancée all but accuses me of being with him, then my fingerprints are on the weapon that was mine. I bought it. It belonged to me. I was using it for my house décor. Can't a girl decorate her house if she wants to? Can't I make my cottage look nice if I decide to have a guest over? Just because I'm not buying cases of champagne doesn't mean I'm not classy. I'm classy enough to not murder anyone, Gary. I may not be Mrs.-Peacock classy, but I know better than that."

Gary put his thick hand on her shoulder before she got in the car. "Look, I know and you know you didn't do anything. Reporters are going to look to you for any kind of information they can twist and turn into a scandal. Sex sells, and unfortunately, Matthew Spencersmith was a playboy. You, my dear, are probably going to be lumped in with his female conquests just because of where he found."

"Ugh. Are you kidding? You can't issue a gag order or a restraining order or something?" Maggie begged.

"I can't do that. But what I can do is keep an eye on your place and make an example of anyone, including Oscar Durham, who thinks they can trespass to harass you. Sound okay?" he asked as he held the car door open for her.

"Yeah," Maggie sighed before climbing in. "Thanks, Gary. You're good people."

Had Maggie not driven out of the parking lot so quickly and with all the windows up she might have heard Gary mutter the words "Anything for you." As it was, her mind was swirling around trying to process everything that had happened since she got up to go to work. It was like she'd been driving all day long and gotten nowhere. Her back hurt, and a headache was creeping in. She'd lost her appetite a while back, and it hadn't returned. She was going to lock the doors, pull the curtains shut, hit the shower, and go to bed early.

Thankfully, as soon as her head hit the pillow, she was asleep. But when she woke up, her day started almost as strangely as the day before had.

# Chapter 6

Now that Joshua had fixed the lights over the display windows, Maggie was able to get started on her next display. It was a tribute to all the green thumbs in Fair Haven who participated in or appreciated the garden walks and flower displays that were popping up all over town. Mrs. Peacock was in an ongoing rivalry with her greatest frenemy, Mrs. Donovan, over who had the better garden. Although Maggie would never say it, she did believe that while Mrs. Peacock's lawn was exquisite, she had landscapers maintain the grounds. It wasn't like she was out there on her hands and knees planting bulbs or pulling weeds. Mrs. Donovan, on the other hand, tended her own garden with the help of a boyfriend who was even older than she was.

As usual, Maggie's shyness required she work alone and behind two canvases. One canvas covered the window. The other kept her creation from prying eyes in the store.

"Knock, knock," Babs said to Maggie, who was behind her curtain.

"Yes?" Maggie peeked out like she was in the shower, holding the tarp across her body with just her head sticking out. She wrinkled her nose and quickly pushed up her glasses.

"I just got a phone call from Old Lady Peacock. Were you expecting a call from her?" Babs asked as she looked down at the pink Post-it note covered with her loopy handwriting.

"No," Maggie replied and stepped out from behind the curtain.

"Well, she just called and asked if you could meet her at St. Jerome's Cemetery in the east wing of the mausoleum." Babs frowned. "Does she ask you to meet her there often?"

"Never," Maggie said and took the note. "Did she say what for?"

Babs shook her head. "She didn't leave a number either. She just asked if you could meet her there around six because she needed to talk to you about something. You know Mrs. Peacock. Always in a hurry." Babs chuckled. "Hey, maybe she wants to discuss leaving that adorable little cottage to you in her will. Or maybe she wants you to have the whole kit and caboodle."

Now it was Maggie's turn to chuckle. "I doubt that. She's taking it all with her when she goes. She told me so."

"I believe you," Babs said before turning back to the café. "Hey, have you seen Casper around? I need his help with a squeaky cabinet door that sticks."

"Yeah. He's fixing a shelf in the stockroom. I'll go get him," Maggie said.

"No, you stay. You've got to get that display ready. I just can't wait to see what you've done this time." Babs smiled and left for the stockroom to find Casper. He'd been working at the bookstore almost since the day Joshua took over. A quiet young man, reliable and sweet. He was an invaluable asset recently, especially over the past couple of days. Joshua had only flickered through the shop, and when he was there longer, he was distracted and busy.

Part of Maggie wanted to ask if there was a

problem. She would have loved to sit down and offer him a sounding board over a cup of tea or a glass of lemonade. In her head when she thought about opportunities to talk to him, she envisioned herself listening intently and offering sage advice that would dazzle him and endear her to him at the same time. In reality, every time the opportunity came up to talk quietly together, she froze up, stuttered, and blathered something about being out of toilet paper or gift boxes. Never coming close to an invitation to talk.

This would have been a perfect opportunity to chat with him about something personal, as Maggie was struck by Mrs. Peacock's request. It wasn't like the old woman had to travel far to see Maggie. But if there was one thing Maggie had learned about her landlord, it was that she did have a flair for the dramatic. Meeting her at the mausoleum was strange but not strange for Mrs. Peacock. There was probably some kind of issue with her late husband's final resting place. Maybe he was complaining about the neighbors to Mrs. Peacock in her dreams. The thought made Maggie giggle.

When six o'clock rolled around, Maggie was at St. Jerome's. She'd paid extra attention to the cars and drivers as she drove, hoping she wasn't being followed by Oscar Durham or his ilk. Although she was no surveillance expert, she was pretty sure she'd not been tailed.

Thankfully, it stayed lighter longer, and the sun was still out at six, lazily inching its way toward the horizon. After she parked her car along the main entrance road, Maggie walked the rest of the way. There wasn't an actual parking lot at St. Jerome's Cemetery unless mourners wanted to use the dry cleaner's lot across the street from the main entrance. But Maggie didn't figure on being there too long, and she was, after all, meeting Mrs. Vivian Peacock. No one would ever dream of telling the wealthy widow that she needed to follow the rules just like everyone else. However, Maggie noticed as she climbed the couple of steps to the mausoleum that Mrs. Peacock's Cadillac was nowhere in sight.

She must have parked somewhere on the grounds. Perhaps she had other people she wanted to visit. Maggie looked around again and saw only one car, and that was a hearse parked off to the side of the mausoleum.

Maggie had not been in the mausoleum before. It looked like it did in every horror movie that took place in a mausoleum. The floors were smooth-as-glass marble polished to a high shine. The windows depicted beautiful religious scenes and symbols in stained glass. White votive candles flickered softly. The walls that weren't covered in subdued shades of marble with bronze placards and flower holders were a soft eggshell color.

"Can I help you, miss?" came a soft voice from behind her. Maggie whirled around to see a man dressed in a security uniform.

"Oh. You scared me." Maggie put her hand to her chest and wrinkled her nose before pushing up her glasses. "I'm supposed to meet Mrs. Vivian Peacock here. Have you seen her?"

"Who?" the man asked softly.

"Vivian Peacock. I think her husband is here. I mean, in the walls. I mean, he was cremated. He's not actually in the walls. You know, he passed away. A while ago," she blathered.

"If you are here to visit a loved one, the mausoleum will be closing in ten minutes," the guard said politely and motioned for Maggie to proceed.

"You didn't see a woman with red hair, probably in a colorful outfit with lots of jewelry?" Maggie asked. The man continued to smile kindly but shook his head. Maggie grinned and shrugged as she stepped further into the building. Her steps made a pat-pat-pat sound as she took a left down the first corridor. There was no one there except for the residents in their vaults. None of them were making a peep. She took a right at the next corridor, and the only thing to make it look any different from the one she just walked down was a bouquet of fresh flowers in a brass vase attached to one of the placards. Maggie walked up and read the name. Paul H. Klingleschmidt. 1938 to—there was no death date.

Maggie squinted at it and wondered what that was all about. Had the survivors run out of money to have the date added? Maybe they didn't want to remember the date. Maybe they didn't like the guy and thought they'd save a few bucks leaving the date off. It's not like Paul would know. Maggie shrugged and kept walking before she took another left. There were several empty folding chairs in front of a vault that had yet to be sealed. Maggie chewed her bottom lip and was about to turn around and go back the way she came when she saw something on one of the chairs. A book.

Maggie looked over her shoulder to see if anyone was around before she picked up the book. At first, she thought it was a little strange for someone to be reading a book at a funeral service.

As much as she loved to read, Maggie knew some things were just plain rude. Then she looked at the title.

"*Death Is Now My Neighbor*. Colin Dexter," she muttered and opened the book to the introduction and gasped. There was a receipt from The Bookish Café. Maggie looked over her shoulder again. This must be a coincidence. The Bookish Café was the only bookstore in town. The chances of someone buying that book and leaving it here were high.

"Who are you kidding? You don't believe in coincidences," Maggie replied to her thoughts. Suddenly, the hair on the back of her neck stood up. She turned around. No one was there, but she got the horrible feeling she was being watched. Dry mouth set in. Part of her wanted to run, but another part of her wanted to prove she wasn't scared. This was a new feeling for her. A confrontational feeling. An aggressive feeling. The feeling that if whoever left this book intended it for her, they should at least have the guts to drop it in her lap on purpose, face-to-face.

"Wait a minute. Maybe Mrs. Peacock left it for you. This might be the vault of a person she knew. You were supposed to meet her here, after all," Maggie whispered. "Maybe she had it on her shelf or someone at her party gave it to her and she didn't want it. Yes. Of course Mrs. Peacock left it for me. So, where is Mrs. Peacock?"

Maggie's gut began to twist again. As ready as she was to accept a reasonable explanation for why this particular book was at the mausoleum, Maggie couldn't shake the feeling this was some kind of setup. Why would Mrs. Peacock ask to meet here? She lived on her property. She could walk to her cottage and talk to her about anything. She'd done it a million times.

That thought triggered an overwhelming sense of fear in Maggie. She clutched the book to her chest, sweat making her palms stick to the cover. Without letting herself get too panicky, Maggie turned and hustled away from the chairs and open vault. But once she rounded the corner, she wasn't sure which way to go. Had she turned right or left? Everything looked the same. There were no distinguishing markings. Not even letters or numbers on the walls like they do at hotels.

"A person steps off the elevator and right in front of them there are numbers with arrows pointing out what is where. Why wouldn't they do the same here? What if I was looking for someone in the walls? How would I find them? This is not a good setup they have here. Not a good setup at all," she muttered. It was the word *setup* that rang in her head. She'd been set up, and now she was lost. Whoever was at the root of this was probably watching her, like a spider watches a fly circle around its web just waiting for it to get stuck so it can pounce.

With each step she hoped to turn the corner and see the security guard, looking annoyed that she was making him late to close the place. But every corner revealed another row that looked just like the one before it.

Finally, Maggie stopped, took a deep breath, and listened. There was nothing. No music. No conversations. Even the sounds from outside were completely silenced by the thick walls of marble and stained glass. Suddenly, the lights at the far end of the corridor started to shut off. Closer and closer the darkness came. Maggie had no choice but to dart off in the opposite direction. That was when she was sure she heard footsteps. Were those her own footfalls echoing back at her? Or was someone coming up behind her? She couldn't stop herself from trying to see over her shoulder. The darkness was closer, and she was almost positive there was someone else hurrying up to catch her, arms stretched out, with a gaping maw, but of course, it was completely hidden in the shadows. Just like all monsters and boogeymen were.

That was it. Her nerves had had it. She opened her own maw to let out a shriek for help, but before a single sound could get out, she ran into something solid that caused her to drop the book and stumble two steps backward.

"I'm so sorry, miss," the attendant said. "I thought I saw you leave."

"What? No. I'm still here," Maggie hooted, quickly bending down to get her book and nearly clunking heads with the man as tears of relief and embarrassment filled her eyes. "I'm still here while you're turning off all the lights and getting ready to lock the place up. Don't you do a last check? What if there was someone really mourning who lost track of time?" She clutched the book to her as if it was a security blanket.

"I'm so sorry. I certainly didn't mean to give you a fright. I would have—" the guard started, but Maggie shook her head and pushed past him to the door that was no more than ten paces away. Once outside she wiped her eyes, feeling like a big baby for freaking out. Without taking a second to look around, Maggie hurried to her car, got in, locked the doors, and headed home. It wasn't even dark outside by the time she made it to her front yard. The yellow tape around her part of the yard made her heart sink. A man was dead and someone was playing games with her. She quickly got inside, slammed the door shut, and snapped the dead bolt in place. Just to be on the safe side, she went from room to room to make sure there were no windows left open or forced points of entry. Satisfied she was alone, Maggie dropped the book on her kitchen table, deciding not to think about it until tomorrow. Just like her hero, Scarlett O'Hara.

## Chapter 7

The night brought anything but rest. Once she was in bed, the only thoughts that seemed to stick were of long dark corridors and creepy stained-glass windows. At one point Maggie opened the bedroom window to let a cool breeze in. The thought that someone might be outside was so overwhelming she changed her mind. Five minutes later she was up shutting the window and snapping the lock firmly in place. A couple hours later she kicked the blankets off, but that made her vulnerable to monsters, so she pulled them back up even though she was too hot. Finally, sleep came to her, but when she woke up, she felt like she'd been running all night. While in the shower, getting dressed, before gulping some coffee and after locking her front door, Maggie yawned. But as soon as she headed up the path to her car, a jolt of adrenaline charged through her veins. There was Mrs. Peacock in her garden.

"Hey!" Maggie yelled and waved, but she wasn't smiling as she approached her landlord.

"Good morning, Maggie. Off to work? Oh, I have the feeling I might be going back to work myself. Everything has become so expensive I just don't know how long I'll be able to hang on. I'm on such a tight fixed income that…" she blathered as she carefully snipped the bloom of a rose the size of a softball.

"Good morning, Mrs. Peacock. Did you call the bookstore yesterday and leave a message for me to meet you at St. Jerome Mausoleum?" Maggie blurted it out then stood there waiting for a reply.

Mrs. Peacock straightened and pulled her shoulders back. "Maggie, why on earth would I do that?"

"So, you didn't? Someone you know didn't make the call for you? Maybe misunderstanding something you'd said?" Maggie asked, hopeful that perhaps this could have all been an innocent mistake.

"No, dear. I don't have any reason to go to St. Jerome's, let alone ask you to meet me there. Why?

Has something happened? It's bad enough we've got the police poking around all the time and calling me at all hours of the night to ask questions." Mrs. Peacock rolled her eyes.

"What are they calling you for?"

"Questions. Questions. More questions. It's gotten so that when the phone rings I just get out my guest list from the party and start reading it off again. Such a terrible tragedy, Mr. Spencersmith."

"Yeah," Maggie muttered and wrinkled her nose as she looked at the sidewalk. "Well, I better get to work."

"Plus," Mrs. Peacock continued, ignoring Maggie's attempt to slowly back away from the conversation that she didn't seem to want to end, "as it turns out, there were a few things that were misplaced after the party. I don't want to alarm you, but I'm quite certain the spare key to the cottage is missing."

"What?" This got Maggie to stop.

"Don't fret. I'll call a locksmith within the next day or two if it doesn't pop up. My keys to the shed, and the garage, and the cellar were all on that ring. Normally, I do put that away for safekeeping when I know I'm having guests. But they weren't in the spot I usually hide them. It's the darndest thing. Something tells me they are in the house somewhere. I just need to retrace my steps."

"The key to my house is missing? What am I supposed to do? What if someone uses the key to get in?" Maggie couldn't understand why Mrs. Peacock wasn't more distressed about this. This was an emergency. This was a serious issue. They could both be in danger. She'd seen her landlady fly into hysterics if her tulips weren't blooming by March 20. But the keys to her property were missing after a party where someone was killed, and she acted like it was nothing more than she forgot to pick up milk at the store.

"Oh, one last thing."

"I can't take it," Maggie huffed.

"With everything going on, please don't walk the grounds at night. I'd hate to be half asleep and grab my shotgun thinking you were our murder suspect," Mrs. Peacock said with a wink. Maggie was the only person who knew the old woman kept a loaded shotgun within arm's reach for self-defense.

"Okay. But I haven't been out on the grounds at night," Maggie replied.

"You weren't out there last night? I thought I saw you coming from the street and strolling casually through my chrysanthemums. My only thought was that you'd gone on a date with Officer Brookes and decided to stroll through my flowers," Mrs. Peacock said as if this was something Maggie had done often.

"A date with Gary? Why would you say that? I didn't go on a date with Gary. Why would you think I did? Did he say something to you suggesting we did? Because we didn't. Not that there is anything wrong with the idea. Has he said something to you? Because if he has you should tell me and I should know, don't you think?" Maggie stuttered.

"I have eyes, Maggie." Mrs. Peacock chuckled.

Maggie stood there without a single word coming to mind. Finally, she remembered she had a job to get to. Now she was going to be late, but at least she knew Mrs. Peacock didn't call yesterday. It was a setup to get her to the mausoleum.

After apologizing to her landlord for being so curt and insisting she be notified if the ring of keys was found, Maggie got in her car without an ambush from Oscar Durham or anyone else from the press and drove to the bookshop. The clock nagged her while traffic made her unable to speed due to all the stop lights along the way. Her mind raced as she tried to get past Mrs. Peacock's comment about her and Gary.

Sure, Gary was a sweetheart, and he looked devastatingly handsome in his uniform. But they were friends. Had been friends a long time. Any kind of romantic entanglement would ruin that. She was sure of it. Plus, he was the kind of man who women looked at all the time. He could have his pick. The chances of Maggie being his type were slim to none. She could see him with a woman who worked out at a gym or maybe liked to hunt and fish while wearing a bikini. Maggie was, in her own words, a wallflower.

When she finally reached the bookstore, she saw the open sign had already been flipped and the lights were on. There was also a familiar truck in the Maggie's usual parking space. The sight of it made her dread going in. It was Roger Hawes's truck. Roger Hawes was the owner of a pawn shop in the industrial part of town. At the funeral of Alexander Whitfield, the first thing Roger did was make it clear to Maggie he had no concern for her friend who died. She'd never forget that.

As Maggie approached the store, Roger exited, pushing the front door open with such force it nearly knocked her to the ground. He was a bulky man who resembled an English bulldog. He had jowls that jiggled when he walked and a shiny head. People might not know it looking at him, but he was a very wealthy man. Unfortunately, he thought that wealth bought him the ability to treat people any way he wanted.

"You haven't heard the last of me, Whitfield," Roger barked. "You've got until Friday at noon to make your decision before I start legal action."

"Mr. Hawes, you aren't getting this bookstore. I don't know how many ways I can tell you, but this building is mine," Joshua replied, with a smirk on his lips. As soon as Maggie heard the words *you aren't getting this bookstore*, her heart jerked behind her ribs.

"I didn't want it to come to this. But you left me no choice," Mr. Hawes bellowed as he pushed past Maggie and stomped off. His grumbling and snorting could be heard until he climbed into his truck and slammed the door shut. Maggie stepped inside the bookstore to see Joshua stomping to the small cubby that was the office. On many past afternoons Maggie and Alexander would sit and enjoy a cup of tea he'd brewed on the hotplate. Topics of discussion were as vast as the collection of titles in the store. It was bad enough Maggie's life had become a little lonelier when he had died, but to not have the bookstore, even the updated and trendier bookstore, as a wonderful reminder of her friend, would be too much for her to bear. She hurried to the office to see Joshua sitting at the tiny desk. He wasn't looking through papers or even getting back to work. He was just sitting there staring at the floor.

"Joshua? What was Roger Hawes talking about? Are you thinking of selling the bookstore?" Maggie asked.

"Not today" was his answer. But it didn't bring Maggie any peace.

"What about tomorrow?" She pressed.

"I don't know," he mumbled. "Mr. Hawes seems to think that this building was supposed to be handed over to him after Dad died. He's got no legal claim to it. There is no paperwork stating the property is his or that after a certain time frame it reverts to him. I don't know where this is coming from, but he wants the bookstore."

"He's wanted it for years. I overheard him more than once try and threaten your father into signing it over to him. Even at your dad's funeral, Mr. Hawes asked who was taking over the payments and what was going to happen to the store. He didn't even care that your dad had passed. It was a real spectacle."

"Yeah, I remember," Joshua said.

"You'd tell me if you were thinking of selling the bookstore, right? You'd give me a heads-up, and I wouldn't just come to work one morning with all the locks changed, right?"

"Maggie. I'd never do that," Joshua replied, slapped his hands on his knees, and pushed himself to his feet. "Hey? What's going on with my display window? When can we have the big reveal?"

"Not yet. I'll go work on it now. Joshua, if there is anything I can do to help, I hope you know all you have to do is ask."

Joshua put on a brave face, but Maggie could tell Roger Hawes made him nervous.

# Chapter 8

M aggie was sure she was going to hit a barrier to her creativity as she went to work on the window display. Since the garden walk was on most people's minds these days and the flowers in town seemed to be just as excited as the gardeners who planted them, Maggie wanted a theme that complimented the festivities. Instead of displaying books about gardening and types of vegetation, she collected books with images by the great masters: DaVinci, Van Gogh, and of course, Michelangelo, along with a dozen or more others who didn't just paint flowers, vegetables, and fruit. They adored these simple things with every brushstroke.

It was hard not to get wrapped up in some of

the books, as the first sketches, rough drafts, and designs were as beautiful as the final works. When she looked at the clock, she was surprised to see that it was almost quitting time. A handful of patrons had made purchases throughout the afternoon, but for the most part she was behind the canvas working on her display. With her mind preoccupied with thoughts of the store, Joshua, and her display, she barely recognized the woman who came in just before closing. The bells over the door jingled, and Maggie shouted a welcome from her hiding place. After a few minutes the woman cleared her throat at the register with a handful of books.

"I'm sorry," Maggie said as she wiped her hands on the canvas before approaching the counter. Poe, who had been sleeping in a square of sunshine, got up, stretched, hopped off the windowsill, slinked around the bookshelf labelled Mysteries, and disappeared.

"Don't worry. I could spend another hour here, but I have to get back to work," the woman said. Maggie flinched as she recognized the sound of the woman's voice but couldn't quite place it.

"I'm glad to hear you're enjoying the shop," Maggie replied.

"It's hard to come by a good bookstore these

days. I've just relocated to town and have a feeling this will be a regular hangout from now on. How's the coffee?" the woman asked pleasantly.

Maggie admired the vintage necklace she was wearing of a green piece of glass in an art deco style popular in the 1920s.

"The coffee is good. Babs runs the coffee shop. I don't know how well I'd do if I didn't get her strong black coffee in the morning," Maggie said.

"Oh, nothing better than a hot cup of strong joe and a good book," the woman continued. That comment made Maggie smile.

"You said a mouthful there. I'm sorry, but we are going to be closing in a few minutes, and I don't think the coffee is on anymore. But we open at nine tomorrow."

"Great. My name is Colleen." Suddenly Maggie knew who she was and why she'd seemed familiar. She was the daredevil at Mrs. Peacock's party. The one who was all for breaking into her house.

*She didn't know it was your house at the time. Perhaps she'd had too much to drink,* Maggie's conscience urged. How could someone so simply appeased with a cup of coffee and a good book be a troublemaker? It just didn't seem possible. The two things didn't go together. A person was either a thrill seeker in life or a person who read about thrill seekers. Either way, Maggie couldn't help but find Colleen fascinating.

"Maggie Bell." Maggie extended her hand, and they shook. Colleen also had a very distinct ring with a clunky red ruby and what she could only assume were diamonds around it. It was an unusual piece for someone her age. Maggie guessed they were not more than a few years apart. A ring like this would be considered a cocktail ring and only worn by ladies with a lot more wrinkles than Colleen had.

"Well, Maggie. It was nice chatting with you. I hope to see you again soon. Perhaps you can recommend some good old books. I just love the classics."

"I think I can do that." Maggie smiled as the woman took her purchase, waved, and pushed the door open just as a rushed and disheveled Joshua burst in. He didn't look at Maggie and instead hurried toward the stairs leading to the apartment over the bookstore.

The intriguing bibliophile had left. Shifting around the counter to quickly lock the door and turn the sign to read "Sorry, We're Closed," Maggie shouted to Joshua. "Are you all right?"

Joshua was stomping up the stairs but stopped

when she called out to him. She heard him let out a deep sigh. "Would you like to come up and have a cup of tea?"

Maggie tugged at the cuffs of her sweater. "Sure."

She followed up behind him, and they entered the apartment, shutting the door just enough for Poe to slink his way in and find the water dish that Joshua always left available along with a little dry food to munch on.

"I didn't mean to be so rude," Joshua said as he walked to the kitchenette, filled a kettle with water, and placed it on the hotplate. Maggie could smell the cologne her old boss used to wear still lingering within the walls of the place. His coat still hung on the rack, and his special collection of books was still in its place. Maggie was happy to see that there was no layer of dust on anything. Joshua was tending to the place. The apple didn't fall far from the tree. For although Alexander was a horrible bookkeeper and not the sharpest dresser, he did make sure the things that were of value to him were taken care of. That included Maggie. The thought made a lump form in her throat, but she managed to choke it down.

"What's going on?"

"It's Roger Hawes. The guy just won't stop."

"Oh, gosh. Has he taken legal action like he said?" Maggie put her hand to her stomach.

"That's just it. The place is mine. It's cut and dry. But he keeps popping up everywhere I go. First, he'll be nice and say things like 'glad the business is going good' and 'just keep in mind my offer.' Then, I'll run into him again the same day, like today, and he'll be threatening me and demanding I talk with him. It's like Jekyll and Hyde."

"That is strange," Maggie said.

"It really is. It's starting to get to a point where I don't want to, but I think a restraining order might be necessary. It's the only thing I can think of. However…" He paused as he stared down at the tea kettle as the steam started to escape the spout.

"However, what?"

"However, I think if he is served with a restraining order, he might really come unglued."

After having Roger Hawes nearly bulldoze over her the other day, she had to nod in agreement. There was no telling what he might do. But still, Joshua had to protect himself and the store.

"Oh, here I am blubbering about something that didn't happen. A bunch of what-ifs. How are you doing, Maggie? How's the display coming?" Joshua said as he held up a tea carton in each hand.

Apple cinnamon and Earl Grey. She pointed to the apple cinnamon.

"I'm fine. I mean, the display is coming along, and I think it will look pretty good. I've got a couple things I'm missing that I think I can pick up at the thrift store to fill in some empty spaces, but all in all it ought to be pretty good. So, yeah, it's coming along pretty good."

*Margaret, you sound like a kid trying to spit out what she wants for Christmas to Santa Claus. Get ahold of yourself.* She took the cup he handed to her and quickly focused on dipping the tea bag in the hot water.

"You really do have a knack for that. Have you ever thought of becoming a professional window dresser?"

Maggie's heart dropped. "Why would I want to do that?"

"I don't know. You're really good at it." Joshua shrugged.

"I know a lot more about books than I do window dressing. Plus, I like the bookstore. I know my way around, and I know a lot of the people that come in. I might not chitchat with people willy-nilly, but that doesn't mean I don't know my books. Even the trashy ones." She sipped her tea and winced as it burned her tongue. Still too hot.

"Those trashy ones are selling, wouldn't you agree?" Joshua said and blew on his cup of tea.

Maggie took a deep breath and smiled. "Yes," she replied.

"You hate it when I'm right." Now it was Joshua's turn to smile. He looked so handsome. Why couldn't he have been a nerdy, overweight eccentric like his father instead of Mr. July in a calendar of muscular bookstore owners? Maggie felt her cheeks heat up and took another scalding sip of her tea before just shaking her head. For a few seconds they sat in silence before Joshua started talking about some new things he wanted to add to the store. A few new bookshelves, as the inventory was getting crowded. He talked about how good the café was doing and that Babs might need another hand soon. The conversation drifted to a few random topics, and Joshua told a few stories about his dad. Before she knew it, she'd been sitting there for over an hour. She'd finished her tea but held on to the cup as if letting it go might lead to the conversation ending.

"You really are an asset to the store, Mags. I want you to know that." Joshua looked at her seriously. "I just don't ever want you to feel... chained down."

"I don't think there is another place in Fair Haven or anywhere else that would overlook my quirks and habits like this place does." She wanted to tell him The Bookish Café was her home away from home. Everyone who worked there was like her family. But she didn't. Instead, she pretended to take another sip of tea.

"Mags, I want to ask you something. Something important. Do you promise not to laugh or scream or go running out of the room?" Joshua said as he leaned forward in his seat.

Maggie tilted her head to the right.

"I've been wanting to ask you this for a while and…"

Maggie leaned forward too. What had he been wanting to ask her? Dare she think it was something romantic? Something she felt too? Maybe he just wanted to know if she'd work a couple extra hours. That was probably it. Sure it was. A handsome guy like him wouldn't want anything from an introvert like her. Every young woman who walked in the place made eyes at him. He probably had one of those little black books filled with the phone numbers of girls he'd dated. Meanwhile, Maggie had a phone book that hadn't had a new number added to it since she changed dentists two years ago.

That reminded her she needed to make an appointment for her six-month checkup.

"What is it?" Maggie asked before pushing her glasses up on her nose.

Just as Joshua was opening his mouth to speak, their conversation was interrupted by a deafening bell. They looked at each other with wide eyes. Maggie lifted her hands, palms to the ceiling with her shoulders hunched.

"That's the burglar alarm!" Joshua shouted and dashed for the door, but not before grabbing a Louisville slugger he had propped against the doorframe. Maggie took off after him, hurrying down the steps as Joshua took them two at a time on the way down. He stopped at the bottom and looked around. Maggie stopped too and saw the same thing he did. Nothing. No broken glass. No jimmied front door. But there was a strange smell that made her heart take off.

"Do you smell that? Is that smoke?" Maggie yelled.

Joshua froze and sniffed the air. He ran to the café but returned with a shrug before heading off to the storeroom.

"Oh no!" he shouted. Maggie ran down the rest of the stairs and to the storeroom. Joshua was standing there with the back door wide open, revealing a blazing fire in the alley. She slapped her hand over her mouth then turned and ran to the cubby that was the office. Within seconds she'd reached the 911 dispatch and gave her name and address and finally yelled there was a fire in the alley behind the bookstore.

"Do you know how fast these books will go up if the building catches?" Maggie cried. Sweat coated her body, not from the heat but from the fear that was swimming through her bloodstream. Her hands were slick against the phone receiver. She licked her lips, but they felt cracked. There was a shushing sound coming from the storeroom. Maggie stretched the cord on the old phone as far as it would go and saw Joshua keeping the fire away from the building with a fire extinguisher only meant to put out a fire on a gas stove or maybe in a barbeque pit. Off in the distance, Maggie was sure she could hear sirens. When she turned and looked out the front windows, she saw the reflection of red and blue lights that were brighter as they approached. The dispatcher was still speaking, but Maggie hadn't heard her. She was replying in gibberish, she was sure of that.

Finally, the rumbling fire trucks pulled up,

making the building shake as they came to a stop in front of the alley. Joshua came back inside to stay safely out of the way, shutting the door behind him.

"Vandals. Someone thinking it would be funny to light the dumpster and garbage on fire." He scowled.

"Did it burn the building?"

"I don't think so. But it came close," he said as he wiped his forehead with his arm. He coughed for a few seconds before he focused on Maggie.

"What are you thinking?" she asked.

Since his eyebrows were pinched together but no words were coming out of his mouth, Maggie was shocked when he stretched out his hand to her. She took it, and they proceeded outside to watch the excitement. A couple of curious onlookers stretched to see the commotion. Several cars slowed down to try and get a glimpse. Maggie and Joshua stood out of the way at the entrance of the alley. Had the building been burned at all? Did the back door get damaged? Before either of them could imagine the worst-case scenario, the firemen shuffled out, their hats off, their uniforms smokey, and their boots wet.

"Fire's out." The firefighter had the name Kelley on his bulky flame-resistant jacket. "We could smell gasoline right away. This fire was deliberately set. We'll send our investigator over as soon as possible." He reached his hand out to Joshua, who nodded absently. He had let go of Maggie's hand for an instant but quickly took it again and squeezed it as he looked down at her.

"Intentionally set? I only know of one person who would intentionally set a dumpster fire just close enough to the building to give us a scare." He scowled.

"Joshua, you don't think Mr. Hawes had anything to do with this, do you?" Maggie asked. Her chest tightened. How many times had he come into the bookshop to hassle Alexander about the business and selling out to him? Too many to count. He was a bully and a blowhard. But was he an arsonist?

"I wouldn't rule it out," he snapped. After a few minutes the investigator for the fire department arrived and began to ask Joshua a million questions.

Maggie had had enough excitement for the night. She left Joshua to handle things while she headed home. She had a lot to think about. But there was another incident. This time at Maggie's cottage.

## Chapter 9

As soon as she walked in the door, something didn't feel right. Maggie stood there for a second, held her breath, and listened. After several long seconds there were no unfamiliar sounds like someone was in the house. But there was a ripple in the air like something had disturbed the smooth surfaces just enough to make it noticeable. That was when Maggie saw it. Two of her books in her bookshelf were out of order. She always kept *Gone with the Wind* by Margaret Mitchell next to *Cat on a Hot Tin Roof* by Tennessee Williams. *Gone with the Wind* was always first. Not now. Now, *Cat on a Hot Tin Roof* was before the epic. Maggie looked in the kitchen and saw a teacup had been shifted from its normal place on her counter.

"This is too much," she mumbled. Perhaps she did absentmindedly put the teacup on the right side even though she's right-handed and holding the teapot full of hot water in her left hand was awkward and difficult and she never did it. Just like she never rearranged her books. Then she realized her door hadn't been locked. Without thinking she'd just walked right in, too distracted by the fire to even realize it.

The memory of Mrs. Peacock informing her of her spare key being stolen prompted Maggie to rush out of her cottage and charge up to the main house. Before she could start pounding on the back door and ringing the bell, Mrs. Peacock appeared, a smile on her face and something in her hand.

"My goodness, Margaret. Are you all right? You look like you've seen a ghost," the landlady said as she stepped out of her house. "I have your new keys here. The locksmith just finished up before you got home from work."

"Mrs. Peacock, did you go in my house while my lock was being changed? It's okay that you did. I just need to know." Maggie panted.

"I let the locksmith in. He needed to have access

to each side of the door." Mrs. Peacock chuckled. "But I've dealt with him a dozen times. He's a very honest and reliable locksmith. He's had a shop in Fair Haven for over twenty years. Surprisingly, he's made a very comfortable life for himself. A lifelong bachelor. His name is Dale. Very nice man."

Maggie rolled her eyes. "Mrs. Peacock, did you or anyone go in my house and look around?"

Mrs. Peacock suddenly acted like the mere question offended her. But she didn't yell or snap. Instead, she looked at Maggie. "No, dear. I did nothing of the sort."

"Someone was in my house, Mrs. Peacock. Whoever took your spare keys has been in my house." Maggie felt tears stinging her eyes.

"Come now. I've been home all day. I didn't see anyone on the property," Mrs. Peacock said. Still, her eyes were focused. Worry lines deepened on her forehead. "Except…"

"Except?" Maggie breathed.

"Mrs. Donovan called and said she had purchased from a thrift store the exact vase I'd purchased from a dealer. Well, of course, I had to go and look at the piece, and as I predicted, it was a fake. She has such an obsession with keeping up with the Joneses. It's rather comical to think—"

"Mrs. Peacock. That means someone was in my house." Maggie couldn't stop the tears from rolling down her cheeks. It was also the only thing that stopped Mrs. Peacock from blathering on about herself.

"Come, dear. Let's have a look." With her head held high and her muumuu flowing elegantly with each determined step, Mrs. Peacock marched to the cottage as if she were going to war. She stepped over the threshold, stood in the living room, and surveyed the miniature estate.

"I know someone has been here," Maggie started as she wiped her cheek with the hem of her sleeve. She pointed out the books, the teacup. Once in her bedroom she noticed a photo on the wall was crooked, and she knew it wasn't this morning when she left.

"Has anything been stolen?" Mrs. Peacock asked firmly.

With her hands on her hips, Maggie saw her first edition books were still in place and her book on France that doubled as a small safe with a lock was also still in place. It held a vintage engagement ring that had been her mother's and five hundred dollars in emergency cash.

"I don't think so," she muttered.

"Dear, are you sure you didn't accidentally move your books or the teacup? I just don't know if that is enough to say for sure that someone had let themselves in," Mrs. Peacock said softly. She wasn't being dismissive. She was being practical. Maggie began to doubt herself. Between the fire and the murder in her front yard and the other things happening over the past couple of days she'd not realized the toll it was taking on her.

"Maybe" was all she could think to say.

Mrs. Peacock took a deep breath and let it out slowly. "I still think a call to the sheriff's office might be a good idea. I'll call from the house. You stay put."

"I'm not going anywhere." Maggie harumphed. Was she losing her mind? Was the stress of the situation getting to her more than she was even aware? Suddenly she felt like she'd run a marathon and needed to sit down. She sat in the seat by the window where she'd first seen Matthew Spencer-smith and his entourage.

Suddenly, Maggie sat up straight. Could this be the work of Mona Plum, the disgruntled fiancée of the budding politician? It made sense. She was the only one who made it very clear she had a bone to pick with Maggie. She all but threatened her outright. It was just a few minutes before the Fair Haven police car pulled up on the gravel drive behind her Dodge Neon. Maggie was so grateful it was Gary who stepped out of the car. She wondered if Mrs. Peacock had requested he be the investigating officer or if it was just the luck of the draw. Either way, Maggie immediately felt better as she opened the door and invited him in.

Gary was even bigger in his uniform and bulletproof vest and seemed to fill up the entire front room. Maggie didn't waste any time. She rattled off her suspicion that someone had been in her house. She acknowledged that she could be mistaken but highly doubted it. The missing spare keys and the people at the party were too much of a coincidence.

"And you know I don't believe in coincidences, Gary. Plus, Mona Plum's behavior at the bookstore is too much not to link together. Come on. Tell me I'm wrong." Maggie sighed. She placed a bottle of water in front of Gary on the kitchen table. He made the front room seem smaller, but the kitchen was downright puny when he was sitting in it. Maggie felt as safe as a kitten.

"I'll say it's strange. I can see where you'd tie the two together," Gary mused.

"I feel a *but* coming on," Maggie snapped.

"*But* I can't arrest someone based on *strange*." He shook his head.

"I'm not asking you to arrest anyone. I'm just thinking if you show up to ask a few more questions you might scare her enough to make her stop. Politely nudge her to move on and find someone else to bother. Is that asking too much?" Maggie shrugged, knowing her friend not only couldn't but *wouldn't* muscle someone unnecessarily. Before he could answer, there was a knock on the door.

"You are expecting someone?" Gary asked.

Maggie shook her head. She walked quietly to the door and peeked outside to see an all-too-familiar and unwelcome face. She gave Gary a quick look and a shake of her head, and the policeman got up out of his chair and stealthily slipped in front of Maggie.

When she backed up, he took a deep breath before yanking the door open with one hand and reaching out with the other to grab a startled Oscar Durham by the collar and give him a good shake.

"What are you doing here?"

"W-What are you doing here?" Oscar stuttered back.

"Let's just call it community outreach. You're trespassing on private property. I could arrest you for that if Miss Bell wanted to press charges. What do you think, Mags?" Gary said, still holding fast to Oscar's collar. The man was no match for Gary, so he just sort of hung there as sweat started to glisten at his temples and over his lip.

"I just wanted to ask her a couple questions," Oliver replied. "She is a suspect in a murder after all."

"What? I'm not a suspect!" Maggie huffed.

"I think you are. Since there is an eyewitness account of Mr. Spencersmith sneaking over here just hours before his body was found." Oscar smirked. He had a greasiness about him that didn't just come with being a reporter. He would be sleazy no matter what kind of job he had. Maggie felt her blood boil, and she took a step closer to him as Gary held on.

"An eyewitness? Who? Who told you they saw… Wait a minute." Maggie gasped. "I know who you've been talking to. Mona Plum. She's the one feeding you this line of malarky. I never saw her fiancé before the night he was killed. I had nothing to do with it, and—"

"What caused the fire outside the bookstore tonight?" Oscar again smirked.

"What? I don't know. The fire chief has an

investigator on the scene. How did you know about it? Maybe because you had something to do with it? Maybe you and Mona are in cahoots. What are you hoping to gain? Money? I don't have any. Fame? I don't have any of that either. So that means you are just a couple of drama queens looking to stir up trouble with the person you think is least likely to stand up to you. Well, you're wrong there."

Maggie was sure she blacked out for a second as another part of her took over and spoke. Where that tough talk and attitude came from, she wasn't sure. But she could tell that she said the right thing by the smirk falling from Oscar's lips and reappearing on Gary's.

"No one is in cahoots. You're paranoid," Oscar replied before Gary gave him a good shake that landed him stumbling off the front porch.

"Maggie, do you want to press charges?" Gary asked.

"I'm just doing my job. I came over here to ask a few questions, not get harassed by the police," Oscar blubbered as he backed up, making sure he was out of Gary's reach.

"You go tell Mona Plum that if she says another word about me, I'll have a lawyer on her for slander and the only hope she'll have for a happily-ever-after is if one of her prison guards springs her from the joint!" Maggie shouted.

She was sure she knew what those overcome by the Holy Spirit felt like when they spoke in tongues. Where those words came from, she wasn't sure, but she was standing by them. Oscar had heard enough and while mumbling to himself hurried off the property down the long driveway to the street before he disappeared behind the shrubbery.

"What has come over you?" Gary said, shaking his head.

"I don't know." Maggie shifted from her right foot to her left as she put her hands on her hips. "But I'm kind of liking it."

"Me too." Gary chuckled.

After waiting around for another half an hour or so, Gary told Maggie he was going to leave but that he'd make sure to cruise past a couple times during the night. Maggie wanted to talk to Mona Plum. But how was she going to do that? It was obvious the woman hated her without any solid reason why. Still, if she could come to Maggie's place of employment and question her then maybe Maggie could do the same. No. Maggie would do the same. Now, how to find out where she worked?

# Chapter 10

There was no listing in the phone book for a Mona Plum. She was a guest of Matthew Spencersmith's at Mrs. Peacock's party, so Mrs. Peacock didn't have an address for her either. The thought of calling Gary and asking him to run her name through their town registry to get her details did cross Maggie's mind, but she knew he wouldn't do it. He was a good, honest cop. He didn't do favors. Although Maggie had never asked him for anything before, she was afraid he might think her request was sneaky. However, if anyone was being sneaky, it was Mona Plum. She had a reporter chasing Maggie, who had it in his head that she was some kind of home-wrecker. The whole thing was disgusting and made

Maggie's stomach turn. Especially since she was sure that Mona had something to do with the fire behind the bookstore.

"Now don't go getting ahead of yourself. You don't know that for a fact," she muttered as she smoothed Poe's fur as he lazily lay on the top of a low bookcase. "But who else would it be, right?" she whispered to the cat.

Just then a familiar face stepped into the bookstore. It was a rare person who came in that brought a smile to Maggie's face. Anyone else might be lucky if they got a nod or a squint of recognition. But seeing Colleen was different. As it turned out, Colleen seemed just as happy to see her.

"Hey, stranger." She waved. Maggie waved back as she approached the front door. Poe, having adequately judged the new person in his vicinity, hopped down and slinked away to perch somewhere in the bookstore where he could quietly observe.

"Hi, Colleen," Maggie replied. The wheels were instantly turning in her head.

*Of course! Colleen probably knows where Mona works. They were at the party together. Small talk dictates you find out what a person does for a living. Right?*

Maggie didn't want to act suspicious, so she

engaged in enough small talk herself to keep the conversation light. But as luck would have it, Colleen was the one who broached the subject first.

"I heard you had a fire last night. I listen to the police scanner. A habit I picked up from my uncle," she said, rolling her eyes and smiling. "I know it's an old lady thing to do but I just can't help myself. I get such a kick out of it."

"You don't have to explain to me." Maggie shrugged. "I always found those things and police work in general to be fascinating. Yup. Someone's idea of a joke. The sad thing is I think I know who did it."

"Really? Did you tell the police?"

"Yes. But they said they won't go talk to this person on just a hunch." Maggie shrugged again and pushed her glasses up on her nose.

"Who do you think it is?" Colleen asked while leaning in a little closer to keep the juicy bit of gossip between the two of them.

"Mona Plum," Maggie said softly, lowering her chin and raising her eyes.

Colleen didn't seem to be surprised. "You know what? I could see it. Didn't you say she came in here raising Cain and threatening you the other day? I've cut loose people who've done lesser things. Did you tell the police?"

"Making threats after your fiancé was murdered isn't considered out of the ordinary, I guess," Maggie replied. "On one hand I feel terrible for her. But I didn't have anything to do with Matthew Spencersmith dying. Let alone have an affair with him. She's wrong. And I want to talk to her. Just talk. Clear the air a bit."

"Well, I wish you all the luck in the world," Colleen said.

"You don't happen to know where she works, do you? She didn't mention it when she was accusing me of adultery." Maggie held her breath and waited.

Colleen scratched her head and looked off in the distance for a couple seconds. Then she snapped her fingers. "If I remember right, she said she works at her father's office as a psychiatrist."

"You're kidding. She's a psychiatrist? She's helping people with their mental health?" Maggie didn't mean to let her opinion just fall out of her mouth that way. But when Colleen giggled, she couldn't help but smile too.

"You know, I'm not claiming to understand it. I

just know she mentioned something about it at the party. Her father was a psychologist, and she had her own clients as a psychiatrist. I'm pretty sure she said her office is somewhere in Logansport. I couldn't tell you the difference between the two professions." Colleen rolled her eyes. "I'm not that educated. But I'm working on it. Speaking of education, can you recommend anything that *wasn't* on the *New York Times* Best Seller list?"

Maggie was thrilled at the request. She led Colleen around and pointed out several titles that she'd read and enjoyed. Colleen picked out three of them.

After a little more chatter about the books, Maggie's vintage pin, and Colleen's eclectic outfit, Maggie was not just happy that Colleen had given her a tip about Mona, but she was genuinely happy Colleen stopped in. They talked a little longer, even after Maggie had flipped the sign to Closed and shut off the soft jazz that played over the speakers mostly in the café.

"I'm sorry. I've kept you long enough. You've got to be dying to get home after a long day. And I've got to meet with family. I'm exhausted just thinking about that," Colleen finally said as she clutched her bag of books.

"Yeah. It was nice chatting with you," Maggie said.

"You too. Let's have coffee sometime. I think we'd have quite a few things to discuss," Colleen said with a smile. "Here's my number."

She scribbled it down and handed it to Maggie, who pushed her glasses up on her nose and slipped the paper into her purse behind the counter.

"That would be fun." Just then Joshua appeared from the back storeroom. Colleen shrugged, waved, and let herself out the front door as Maggie skirted around the counter and snapped the dead bolt shut.

"Who was that?"

"Colleen," Maggie said and gave a quick synopsis of how they met. "I feel kind of bad. I didn't have a very good first impression of her. But she's quite nice."

"Hey, first impressions aren't always the right ones. I thought you were a bossy bookworm and… oh wait," Joshua teased.

Maggie stared at him with no expression as he giggled.

"You're a regular riot, Mr. Whitfield," she finally said, making Joshua laugh all the more. She grabbed her purse and left the shop without uttering another word but relishing in the fact she'd made him laugh. However, she had other more pressing things on her mind. Like finding out where Mona Plum worked.

# Chapter 11

I t wasn't hard. There were seventeen psychiatrists in Fair Haven and the surrounding area. Colleen's tip was spot-on. Only one office was listed in Logansport, about ten minutes away from Fair Haven, and it was listed under Dr. M. Plum.

The only problem Maggie saw was that Mona probably wouldn't take a meeting with her if she knew she was coming. An ambush was the only alternative. Staking out her place of business until she was sure she was alone was her best chance of getting her to listen to Maggie's side of things. The office was located in a cold-looking building that was home to several businesses including a dentist, two lawyers, a dietician, and an accountant.

Maggie couldn't help but think it was a collection of the most boring professions in a boring building. The plants in the unmanned lobby were plastic. The decor was late seventies with orange and olive-green tapestries on the walls. The floor was a bland grayish tile seen in schools. The elevator to the three other floors clanged as it went up and down. Maggie was sitting on an orange ottoman watching the doors and waiting. Even with the sun shining through the glass double doors there was still an aura of dullness around everything.

After waiting about twenty minutes, Maggie was considering leaving when she saw Mona approaching the doors.

*Don't be scared. She came to your place of business first. Let's see how she likes it,* Maggie tried to encourage herself. However, she couldn't help it. She was nervous. She stood up and smoothed her gray slacks and brushed her tan blouse before tugging at the scarf she had around her neck. Then, after pulling up courage from the very bottom of her feet, she stepped in front of Mona.

"Miss Plum, I'd like to speak to you," she said softly.

"Really? I don't have anything to say to you. Do you think this is cute, coming to my office? Is that how you met up with Matthew? Hmm? Did you two meet at his office or did you sneak out to little out-of-the-way places where no one would recognize you?"

"You really have this all wrong. I never met your fiancé before in my life. You are going after the wrong person. Sending Oliver Durham to question and harass me is not only wrong but a waste. I'm not your girl. Would I come all this way to talk to you if I was guilty of the things you think I've done?" Maggie watched Mona's expression. For a split second it softened as if maybe she was getting through to her. But, like a switch had been flipped, Mona shook her head and narrowed her eyes.

"I don't know why you are here. Perhaps you have a guilty conscience. Maybe you just love the drama and the attention," Mona scoffed.

"No. I don't. I don't want any attention."

"Come on, Miss Bell. A woman like you suddenly involved in the murder of your lover who was engaged to someone else," Mona hissed. She was crazy. No amount of talking or proof was going to change her mind. "Don't blow smoke at me. This is the closest you've ever come to being important, and you're loving it. That's the only reason you are here. Just know that if you hadn't been having an affair Matthew would still be alive. His death is your fault."

It was no use. Maggie had no experience with someone like Mona. A person so damaged that she not only couldn't but *wouldn't* listen to the truth.

"I'm telling you that I didn't know your fiancé and I am sorry for your loss," Maggie said as she wrinkled her nose and squinted before starting to walk toward the glass doors.

"Tell me this. Why were you spying on the people at that party? You live in that little shack right on the property, but you weren't invited? That didn't make you mad? Your lover is there with his fiancée, and you aren't even invited, let alone asked by him to go. That tells me a lot about who you are without you having to say a word."

"I wasn't spying. I was just sitting—"

"I'm going to find out everything, and when I do, I'm going to burn the whole thing down," Mona hissed.

"Burn?" Maggie muttered as she stood there dumbstruck. Mona stomped off, her head held high as she stepped into the elevator. The doors closed with a thud, and the clanking and groaning up the elevator shaft was the only sound echoing through the sad-looking lobby.

"Maybe I did kill Matthew Spencersmith," she muttered. "Maybe I had some kind of episode and blacked out. I had been annoyed and upset over the whole ordeal. Maybe some part of me did do something bad," Maggie whispered as she walked to her car.

*No. Of course you didn't kill anyone,* her little voice tried to soothe her, but it was drowned out by a bigger voice that was happy to remind Maggie of the cold, hard facts.

*But you were hurt that you didn't get invited to yet another party of Mrs. Peacock's. People thought your home was the work shed. Empty. They were going to smash the windows to get inside. That's enough to make any normal person upset. You are no exception. Admit it. You were mad.*

The tears stung her eyes. Maggie quickly got in her car and scolded herself for coming anywhere near this woman. Mona was a psychiatrist. She knew how to read people and manipulate their feelings. It was her job to decipher what was being said as well as what wasn't being said.

It all made Maggie feel sick to her stomach. When she arrived at the bookstore, her head was pounding. This was the last place she wanted to be, but she had to plow through it. The inventory wasn't going to put itself away, neither was the window treatment going to finish itself. But just when Maggie thought it couldn't get any worse Joshua came from the office with something in his hand.

"Look at this," he said to Maggie, unaware that she wanted to do anything other than talk with people. But she put on a brave face and asked what he had. "This was the only thing that survived the dumpster fire," he said as he presented the charred remains of *The Scarlet Letter* by Nathaniel Hawthorne. Maggie felt panic from the tips of her toes race all the way up her body. She had to talk to someone. Someone who would listen to her and not just blow off what she was saying. She knew it sounded crazy. But Mona Plum was a woman scorned, not just by Matthew Spencersmith but by the women he cheated on her with. No facts, no matter how solid, were going to discourage Mona from her plan of revenge.

However, it was one thing to scare Maggie with wild goose chases. It was another to try and burn the building down. Without further explanation, Maggie told Joshua she wasn't feeling well.

"I know I have to get the window done. I will. But I'm just not myself today. I'm sure I'll be better tomorrow," she said. It wasn't a total lie. But when she said it was probably something she ate, that was a lie.

"Mags, I don't think you've called in sick since I took over the business. Go on home. Take tomorrow, too, if you need it," he said.

Maggie wrinkled her nose and nodded before grabbing her purse and hurrying out of the bookshop. For a moment as she was driving home, she did feel nauseous and contemplated pulling over. But it passed. Inside her cottage she didn't feel any better. It was a mixture of anxiety and depression, and if she were being honest, she was a little hungry. Without knowing what else to do, she pulled Colleen's number from her purse and dialed.

"Hello?"

"Hi, Colleen. Um, this is Maggie. Maggie Bell from The Bookish Café," Maggie chirped, hoping she didn't sound as desperate as she felt.

"Maggie! I was just thinking about you. I'm going to tell you right now that I am loving this book you recommended, *The Butler's Diary*. It is so interesting that I just can't put it down and—"

"I'm glad you like it," Maggie muttered.

"Is something wrong?"

Maggie took a deep breath and spilled part of her story to Colleen before she was interrupted.

"Why don't you come over this afternoon. I'm only about half an hour from the bookstore. I'll put on some tea, and we can dish the dirt. How does four o'clock sound?" Colleen suggested.

Maggie felt a wave of relief and smiled for what felt like the first time in days.

# Chapter 12

When Maggie pulled into the driveway of the bungalow-style home, she was surprised at the simplicity of the house. Colleen had a gazing ball and a wooden windchime adorning the entrance. Before she could make it up the sidewalk, the front door was opened, and her hostess was standing there in sweatpants and a sweatshirt with her hair in a ponytail.

"Did I mention this was a casual day? I'm not putting on pants with a zipper until I absolutely must," Colleen called from the door.

Maggie smiled and waved. As soon as she stepped foot into Colleen's house she was again blindsided by the décor. It wasn't quite what she'd expected. Very minimalist. No portraits or personalized knickknacks. Plus, there was a surprising lack of books for someone who read so much. But the smell of hot chocolate made her quickly dismiss her questions.

"Your house is lovely," Maggie said.

"I'm renting." Colleen rolled her eyes. "Until something comes on the market that I like, I've decided to live here on a month-to-month basis. It's not what I'm used to, but it will have to do."

"What are you used to?" Maggie asked.

"A little bigger." Colleen winked and led her into the kitchen. It was practical, nothing special, but if she was renting Maggie could understand not wanting to plant roots too deeply. She sat down at the table and was suddenly overcome with emotion. Bursting into tears wasn't something she did often. But she could feel their sting and the lump in her throat as she let out a defeated sigh.

"I hope you don't mind hot chocolate. I thought under the circumstances a little comfort food was required." She pulled a raspberry coffee cake from the fridge too.

Maggie smiled as her shoulders drooped. "None of this was necessary. But I'm so glad you did," she replied. After wrapping her hands around the warm mug, Maggie took a sip. It wasn't the greatest hot chocolate in the world. Babs made that. But it was the thought that counted, and at this moment, Maggie was grateful for the effort.

"So. You've got a problem with Mona. Believe me, there is a long line of people who have a problem with Mona Plum. We knew each other in college. We weren't best friends, but I have experience with her. She had a plan to marry well and build her business as a shrink. With a fiancé in politics, she'd for sure have a never-ending list of patients," Colleen said. "My family has filled me in on what she's been up to since I got home. She's wallowing in attention now. As soon as it starts to wear off, she'll sink her claws into another up-and-coming politician type to keep her in the lifestyle she's become accustomed to. I think she really identified with that Mrs. Peacock. A wealthy widow who throws big parties and has everyone sucking up to her. I watched Mona roam through the house, and I swear there was a calculator in her head adding up all the valuables and taking inventory."

"It's just so frustrating. I didn't do anything to her. She's convinced that Matthew and I had some kind of tryst. I've never had a tryst in my life," Maggie confessed, making Colleen laugh. "I tried to talk to her, but she wasn't hearing me. Then, she made a comment that was so… bizarre."

Carefully, Maggie repeated the words about burning and described Mona's demeanor and the look in her eyes.

"That's scary," Colleen said before taking a sip of her own cocoa.

"Do you think I should tell the police? I've got a friend on the police force." Maggie shrugged. The thought of going to Gary again with this made her feel like she was taking advantage of their friendship. Besides, what could he do?

"I'm not sure he'd be able to do anything," Colleen said as if she was reading Maggie's mind.

"Right. You probably know him," Maggie said. "Officer Gary Brookes. I know he had questioned most of the people who were at Mrs. Peacock's party."

Colleen didn't bat an eye.

"He's a big guy. A couple of tattoos. Handsome," Maggie admitted.

Colleen shook her head. "To be honest, I was so shocked at what happened I don't think I was really paying any attention to who was asking me what." She chuckled. "Speaking of handsome, what's the story with the guy who works with you at the bookstore?"

Maggie nearly choked on the last bit of hot chocolate in her mug, making Colleen chuckle as she leaned back in her chair and grinned.

"Joshua? He's the owner, and there is no story. I worked for his father before he died. Joshua kept me on after he took over because I knew how all the day-to-day procedures were done." Maggie went into the details of her years with Alexander, describing him as if he were her own father. There were so many fine memories and funny stories that before long Maggie and Colleen were laughing.

"I think I read every book in that place because of him. He was just one of those old-time gentlemen that don't come around much anymore," Maggie mused as she helped herself to a piece of coffee cake. Colleen did the same. "He was like family. Everyone at the bookstore is like family now. But sometimes—"

"Sometimes you need a different sounding board." Colleen finished Maggie's sentence.

"What about you? You said you were visiting family here? Who is your family? Maybe I know them. Although, I doubt it. I'm kind of a home-body," Maggie replied.

Colleen shook her head, her ponytail waving behind her head. "Hey, I have an idea. You're feeling like Mona has gotten the upper hand. Nothing makes a person feel more helpless than inaction."

"Yeah. That's true," Maggie said as she eyed Colleen suspiciously.

"Let's go to Mona's house."

"And do what? I already tried to talk to her, and she had nothing to say. Actually, she had plenty to say, and none of it was nice. I'm not interested in getting another verbal lashing from her." Maggie squinted as if she was anticipating a smack on the cheek.

"I'm not saying we go try and talk to her. I'm just saying we go and see where she lives. She puts her pants on one leg at a time. She has to clean her windows and buy groceries and use the bathroom just like you and me. Maybe seeing her house will take away some of the mystery and put your mind at ease." Colleen shrugged.

It wasn't the craziest thing Maggie had ever heard. "I don't know."

"She's not some all-powerful sorceress. She'll never even know we were there. Plus, it will get you out in the fresh air. Nothing helps a person think clearer than oxygen to the brain," Colleen suggested.

"Do you know where she lives?"

"I do. My date for Mrs. Peacock's party told me all about her. He was a nice guy. A friend of my uncle's. He needed a date to take, and I had a free night. Boy, of all the nights I should have stayed at home, right?" Colleen chuckled.

Before Maggie could think too hard about the whole situation, Colleen had her purse over her shoulder and was tugging Maggie by the hand toward the door.

"Okay, a quick drive-by but nothing more. I'm still not so sure this is a good idea." Maggie squinted as she let Colleen lead her outside. She let go of her hand to lock the front door and then looked at Maggie.

"Can you drive? My car is in the garage."

"Sure. Can you tell me how to get there?"

"Maggie, I think this is going to help. I feel better for you already." Colleen smiled as she nodded her head. The strange thing was that Maggie was starting to think Colleen had the right idea. The fresh, cool air. The sun starting to set. Nothing pressing waiting for her at home. Why shouldn't she go out for a while and clear her head?

If her adventure took her past Mona Plum's house, so be it. There was no harm in driving around the neighborhood, even if it wasn't Maggie's neighborhood.

"I feel better already too," Maggie admitted as she buckled up and turned the key. The engine sputtered to life, and within minutes they were on their way to Mona Plum's house.

## Chapter 13

"So, you knew Mona in college?" Maggie asked.

Colleen pointed ahead, telling Maggie to turn right at the street with the currency exchange on the corner.

"I had a couple of prerequisites with her. We were cool with each other for a while. But then I had different opinions on certain things than she did. It ended up causing a rift between us that was never healed. We just didn't click anymore." Colleen seemed to be saddened by the situation. Maybe it was she who really needed to take a drive past Mona's house in order to feel a sense of closure or reality or distance. It struck Maggie that maybe they both needed this simple exercise in taking the wind out of Mona's sails.

"When she started dating Matthew, that was when the real end came. She couldn't be associated with someone like me. You can imagine how shocked she was when I showed up at Mrs. Peacock's party. I also think she had a problem with Matthew's roaming eyes. He's no different from any man." Colleen nodded. "I can't help it if he was paying more attention to me."

"You looked really pretty," Maggie said. She would have never been caught in an outfit like Colleen had worn. However, she saw how it did fit Colleen's personality. Colleen was much braver than Maggie was, and Maggie thought that was a wonderful quality.

"Thanks. I might have been a little more party girl than debutante, but that's usually what happens." She chuckled.

As they turned this way and that, the conversation went from clothes to books to movies to exercise and finally to the street they'd been looking for.

"Mona's house is the corner house on the left," Colleen whispered.

"Are you sure?" Maggie asked in a hushed voice as she squinted. It was then she saw a familiar car and a familiar man walking up the driveway to the front door of a quaint Tudor-style house that was perfectly maintained with a lawn as immaculately manicured as Mona's nails had been.

"What? What is it, Maggie?"

"That's the sleazy reporter that was at my house not once but twice to snoop around and ask all kinds of prying questions. Oliver Durham." Maggie squinted as she slowed the car down. Instead of turning left to go around the house, Maggie turned right, drove down a block, and parked the car.

"What are you doing?" Colleen asked.

"I'm going to get a closer look. If she's dealing with that guy, she's not as professional as she pretended to be earlier today."

Just as Maggie reached the house, the streetlights flickered on. Colleen was hurrying up behind her just as she reached a row of bushes in front of the house catty-corner from Mona's. Oliver's car was sitting there in the driveway looking out of place, as its rust spots and one donut tire indicated it didn't belong.

With quick steps she shuffled across the street then slowed her gait as she made her way along the side of the house. A white estate fence encompassed a border of peony bushes that were bursting with pink, white, and maroon flowers. The backyard was as impressive as the front with a raised deck, tall ceramic pots bursting with flowers, a fire pit that was currently glowing softly, and a patio set that could easily accommodate a party of ten. Maggie was sure she didn't know ten people let alone ten to invite to her house for a cookout.

"Have a seat. I want to know what you've found out," Mona said as she stepped out onto the deck, Oliver following close behind her. Maggie held her breath and ducked down low to peek between the fence and peonies.

"I'm telling you again I can't find anything on this girl. She's a real wallflower," Oliver said as he sat down on the edge of the chair across from Mona. He rubbed his hands together between his knees.

"Those are the ones with the most to hide. Do you really mean to tell me that bookworm hasn't left her mark somewhere? She shows up at my office and smarts off. That's not the kind of thing a woman does if she has nothing to hide," Mona said as loudly and plainly as if she were trying to be heard over a crowd at a restaurant. It was painfully clear who she was talking about. Maggie's eyes bugged as she looked at Colleen, who had carefully snuck up alongside of her.

Maggie felt a wave of heat wash over her. The last thing she wanted was for her new friend to hear people speaking so negatively about her. Plus, what did Oliver Durham find out about her? Although she couldn't think of anything she'd done that would be worth repeating, that didn't stop her from panicking. Her hands were clammy as she recalled the time she had too much to drink at a dive bar with Joshua as she tried to collect information on... Oh... she couldn't remember.

"I'm telling you, Mona, there isn't much on this girl. She works at a bookstore and goes home to that little house, and that's it."

"How long was she seeing Matthew?"

"I don't have any proof that she ever did," Oliver protested. "I wasn't able to dig up anything on her. She's just a clerk at the bookstore. Nothing more. Plus, even if I did find something that indicated she was carrying on with Mathew, it doesn't make sense that she would kill him on her property and—"

"It's not *her* property. She doesn't own *anything*. That's Peacock's property," Mona hissed as if there was something wrong with Mrs. Peacock not only having a big piece of land but letting Maggie live on it. She wasn't sure if she wanted to laugh or cry. With her legs folded uncomfortably and her back hunched, Maggie's muscles were starting to protest being in such a position.

"Well, he said he didn't find anything on you," Colleen whispered.

Maggie shrugged as she squinted at the duo on the patio. Of course Durham wasn't going to find anything on her. She didn't do anything but work and read. For a second Alexander popped into her head. He was an old man when she first met him, but he lived a colorful, exciting life in his youth. Often, he told stories of trips he took and people he met. It wasn't like he was some jetsetter who hobnobbed with the who's who. He was just a man who did some travelling when he was young because *The Lord of the Rings* made him want to see J. R. R. Tolkien's birthplace and Mario Puzo's *The Godfather* enticed him to take his new bride to Sicily for their honeymoon. But those were the most exotic places he'd mentioned to Maggie. She had no desire to go to either place. Maybe it was because she figured she could read all she needed to know about these places. Or maybe it was because she was afraid to fly over the ocean.

Suddenly she realized that she wasn't just afraid to fly over the ocean, but she was afraid of changing any bit of her routine. Why didn't she ask Mrs. Peacock to attend her party? That could have saved her a lot of trouble had she been there making small talk and listening to the music from a lounge chair on the terrace instead of in the shadows of her own home, pretending not to be there. What was Mrs. Peacock afraid she'd do? Make a scene? And so what if she did? Would it have been the end of the world?

"You aren't looking hard enough." Mona's voice was louder and snapped Maggie out of her thoughts and back into the moment.

"Mona, I'm telling you that Margaret Bell didn't have any connection to Matthew. Why are you so reluctant to accept it?" Durham retorted.

"Something in my gut tells me she did it. You said they found a hammer with her prints on it. He was steps away from her house," Mona insisted.

"But what is the motive?"

"Jealousy. He was going to marry me. No matter what he told anyone else, we had an agreement, and Matthew was going to marry me. I was the perfect wife for an up-and-coming senator ready to win his first election next November. He couldn't have some frumpy wallflower saddling his campaign. Choosing the correct wife is as important as which university to attend or what internships will get you farthest."

"I'm sorry. I didn't know he bought you a ring," Durham replied. A silence so deafening fell over the pair on the patio that for a minute Maggie thought she'd gone deaf.

"Keep digging. Until you have something I can work with, your check will be held for safekeeping. I'll pay you when you get me what I want," Mona replied pleasantly, but Maggie could see the cold glisten of her eyes from the bushes.

"I have to go to the bathroom," Colleen whispered.

"Just wait a few minutes." Maggie shushed her.

"I'm serious. I can't wait," Colleen said before she turned and headed back toward the car. Maggie bit her lip and was just about to follow her when a big black ant decided Maggie looked as enticing as the peonies.

It wasn't that Maggie was afraid of ants. She wasn't. They were no different from bees or grasshoppers or other crawlies equally harmless. But when a bug fell on her arm and at first glance appeared to be a spider, an arachnophobe like Maggie let out a yelp. It was more like a gasp simultaneous with a sneeze. Add to that a jerky movement to swipe away the creepy thing and it was a perfect storm to give away her location to the people she was spying on.

*Way to be stealthy,* her conscience criticized as she held her breath and watched.

Colleen was already down the street. Where she planned on going to the bathroom, Maggie didn't know. But she couldn't let her get to the car alone and just sit there waiting.

Hunched over with her back still bent and her legs crying out in pain, Maggie slowly eased into a crouching position. But it was too late.

"Hey! Who is that?" Mona shouted from her patio. "Go see who that is," she ordered Durham, who sat back and folded his arms. Maggie could see Mona stand up. Before she could make it to the fence to discover Maggie spying, Maggie dropped to all fours and crawled just far enough to be at the corner of the street before popping up and running to her car. The sound of her knees popping was only eclipsed by the pain she felt after just a few steps. What happened to her? Was she that out of shape that running one city block left her breathless and aching? Maybe all that reading wasn't as good for her as she thought.

By the time she reached her car and dove behind the wheel, Colleen was waiting, anxiously bouncing her knees.

"We'll stop at a gas station," Maggie panted.

"Sounds good," Colleen replied.

It took five minutes for Maggie to peel out and find a gas station for Colleen to use the restroom. As she sat in the car waiting, she thought about what she'd heard. Mona was not going to stop until she dug up something on Maggie. The sad thing was Maggie knew there would be no pot of gossipy gold at the end of the rainbow. Her life was quiet and uneventful.

"It might be now, but it doesn't have to stay that way. Time to shift gears and head down the dirt road for a change," she muttered.

## Chapter 14

Finally, after a few minutes and a couple of deep breaths, Maggie's heart had slowed down and her brain was speeding up. Colleen walked out of the gas station and wiped her brow with a huge smile on her face.

"That was a close one in more ways than one." She laughed as she climbed into the passenger's seat. Maggie laughed, too, then shook her head.

"Thank you, Colleen," Maggie said.

"For what?"

"For getting me to come out tonight and face my fears, sort of."

Colleen smiled. "You're welcome. I told you that Mona Plum isn't anyone to be scared of. Neither is that guy she was talking to. If you were to get in her face and talk to her the way she talked to you, I'll bet she would back off. She's a bully. Nothing stops a bully like a bigger bully."

Maggie thought as she drove back to Colleen's house. Colleen was talking, but Maggie was only half listening as she rewound the things she'd heard Mona saying.

"I think I should tell the police," Maggie said, cutting Colleen off in midsentence.

"And tell them what? That you went to her house after stalking her at work and spied on her like a little kid at her home? Okay," Colleen replied.

"When you say it like that." Maggie frowned and pushed her glasses up on her nose.

"You'd have to tell them I was with you," Colleen said.

"Yeah. I'd tell them, but I don't think that would matter."

"You don't? Think about it. I told you that Mona and I knew each other before and had a falling out. She's such a drama queen that I just know she'd concoct some scandal to make my name mud. Let's face it. That's what she's trying to do to you," Colleen insisted. "I don't think she'll succeed. But that isn't stopping her. Right?"

"Right," Maggie replied. When she'd finally

pulled into Colleen's driveway, she wasn't sure what she should do. But she did know one thing for sure. "I need to use your bathroom. I should have gone at the gas station."

Both ladies giggled as Colleen punched in a code that opened her garage door. Maggie slipped in and admired the nice car Colleen had. It was an Audi, silver in color with gray leather interior. Maggie peeked in the backseat as she scooted past following Colleen to the inside door. In the backseat was a toolbox and some tools.

"I am an amateur do-it-yourselfer. I was hoping to make one of those standing gardens, so the rabbits and critters don't get into it," she said with a smile as they stepped into the kitchen from the garage.

"I would love to know how to do those kinds of things," Maggie said before she quickly found the bathroom.

"Hey, maybe we could do something together some time. That might be fun," Colleen called from the kitchen where she waited. "Of course, don't be surprised if the table ends up wobbly or the picture frame is narrower at one end than the other."

A few minutes later Maggie emerged from the bathroom and strolled into the kitchen. The bathroom, like the rest of the house, had nothing personal except a hairbrush on the sink and an extra roll of toilet paper on the toilet tank. "Where did you learn how to do that kind of handywork?"

Colleen clicked her tongue. "My uncle thought it would be beneficial if I learned how to turn a wrench and tighten a screw. They offered some classes on weekends. I had nothing else to do, so I signed up, and now I know how to turn a wrench and tighten a screw."

Maggie laughed. When she said her good-byes and promised to call Colleen if there were any further developments, Maggie had a weird feeling in her gut. She liked Colleen. But there was something there that she couldn't quite put her finger on that made her seem familiar and foreign all at the same time.

*You're just not used to people. There is a lot to like if you think about it, Margaret. Stop being so paranoid. You had fun with Colleen. Leave it at that,* she soothed herself. *You did something new you normally wouldn't have done. Plus, the fresh air and one-block sprint did your body and soul some good. Stop looking for a boogeyman around every corner,* her conscience hissed as she hugged Colleen and waved good-bye.

But on her drive home she wondered if she

shouldn't tell Gary what she'd done. Not just scoping out Mona's house and what she overheard but also that she tried to talk to her at her job this morning and how the whole experience made her sick to her stomach.

Gary would not be happy with her. No matter what she said or how she legitimized her actions, he would tell her that she put herself in jeopardy and made herself look a bit looney.

"I know what I'll do. I'll sleep on it. I won't do anything until I've had a good night's sleep," Maggie said as she pulled her car into her own gravel driveway. Her little cottage that had been her home for several years was a welcoming sight in the light of the moon.

She felt good about her decision to wait, and that night Maggie slept deep. When she woke up her head was clear, her mind was focused, and she was ready to have a good day. Her decision was that she would tell Gary what she'd done. She'd explain why she did it. There was no need to be scared or bashful about the situation. Besides, no one was looking out for her but her, and she was not going to let Mona Plum get away with saying she had something to do with the death of Matthew

Spencersmith when nothing could be further from the truth.

It was a very convenient coincidence that Gary pulled up in the squad car across the street from the bookstore just a short while after Maggie had flipped the lights on and turned the Open sign around. Her nerves fluttered, but she was going to tell him what she'd found out and that there might be a reason to talk to Mona Plum sooner rather than later. But he appeared to have changed his mind and headed off down the sidewalk past the bookstore in the direction of the bank. Not a wave or a wink or anything.

"That was weird," she muttered to Poe as he got a scratching behind his ears. He'd stretched out along the window ledge as usual and let his tail hang lazily over the edge, flipping every so often with the movement only a content cat showed. Maggie went back to stocking the shelves. New books had arrived from a couple of New York publishers, which meant Maggie would have some stacking and reorganizing to do to remove the old stuff and make room for the new. She dove right in, and the thought of Gary sidestepping the bookstore without even a slight acknowledgment that she was there slipped to the back of her mind. She went over exactly what she was going to tell him about her stakeout at Mona's. The truth. If he needed a witness, she had Colleen. There was no question that Mona was a little unhinged.

After some time had passed, the little bells jingled happily as the door opened and Gary came in. Maggie smiled but immediately could tell her confession might be put on the back burner. She gave him an awkward smile.

"Maggie," he said and cleared his throat. He walked up to her with his back rigid.

"Hi, Gary. You're just the guy I wanted to talk to," Maggie said.

"I need to talk to you too. Can we talk in the office?"

Maggie hadn't seen Gary so nervous or upset ever. He was starting to sweat at his temples, and there was a grimace of worry on his face. Maggie didn't say anything, put down the books she had been holding in her arms, and walked to the small cubby that was the office.

"What's the matter?" Maggie fretted that something had happened at the police station or maybe he'd gotten bad news from home. His parents were still alive and lived about two hours away in Manly Township.

"Maggie, I need you to sit down," he said softly. She did as she was told and took a seat in the old wooden chair that had supported Alexander Whitfield's weight for over ten years. It squeaked in protest.

"What's the matter?"

"Mona Plum is in the hospital." His words echoed like he'd spoken loudly in a church, even though he whispered.

"What?"

"She was attacked last night at her home," Gary said. The look on his face told Maggie that wasn't the end of the story. It felt like the heat suddenly went off, but Maggie was still starting to sweat.

"Last night?"

"Maggie. Someone said they saw you and your car there. Is that true?"

This was not supposed to be how she confessed to spying on Mona Plum. The whole ordeal was supposed to unfold neatly with her explaining to Gary what she did and why. His response was supposed to be one of understanding and sympathy and a promise to get to the bottom of why Mona was so convinced Maggie was to blame for her lover's death. Instead, it was crashing like a trainwreck of circumstantial evidence against Maggie.

"Uh, well, um, technically yes," Maggie stuttered.

Gary rolled his eyes. "Did you accost her at her job yesterday too?"

"Accost her? No! I went to talk to her. I thought that if I could just sit with her for a few minutes, I could find out why she had a bullseye on me and maybe she'd see that I'm no homewrecker. I'm not even in the same neighborhood." Her voice shook, and Maggie felt like she was about to cry. But she took a deep breath and carefully touched Gary's arm. "You gotta know I'd never hurt anyone. After all the years of knowing me, Gary, I'm not that tough."

"Believe me, Mags, I don't think you attacked anyone. But you were there. She's in the hospital and is convinced it was you that broke into her house and…"

Maggie's head began to spin. "Broke in?" She was sure at any second she was going to faint. Before that humiliation could take place, she leaned forward and took a couple deep breaths.

Gary asked her a couple more questions, and she answered everything honestly. There was no reason to lie. She hadn't done anything. Spy? Yes.

Gossip a little? Yes. But did she break into someone's home and hurt them?

"No, Gary. I'd never do that. Not in a million
years," she said as she pulled herself together. This
was not just some awkward social situation. She
didn't have the time to be an introvert and let things
unfold as they would. With her chin raised she looked
square at Gary and shook her head and said exactly
what was on her mind. "Someone is setting me up."

"I couldn't help but think that myself. Who?"
Gary asked quietly.

"It's got to be Mona. If you speak to
Colleen..." Maggie replied as she pushed herself
out of the old chair, which creaked in relief.

"Colleen who?" Gary took out his pocket notebook and a stump of pencil to write with.

Her mind was a blank. Maggie shook her head
and squinted, stamped her foot, and pulled her hair
back from her face. "I don't know. I don't think I
ever asked." But then she snapped her fingers. She
dashed to her purse beneath the register and pulled
out the phone number Colleen had given her as
well as the other paper that had the address scribbled on it. She handed them to Gary, who put them
in his breast pocket.

"I don't think I need to tell you not to go on any long trips or make plans to leave town." Gary smirked.

"This isn't funny." Maggie folded her arms and shifted from her right foot to her left. "Will Mona be okay?" It was strange, but Maggie desperately wanted to know that the woman who seemed to be turning her life upside down was going to pull through. The only thing that would be worse would be if Mona Plum succumbed to this attack and all the while believed it was Maggie who caused it. Maybe that was a selfish way to think of things. Their worlds were so different. Had the roles been reversed, would Mona be so concerned about a nobody like Maggie, who had no connections, didn't go to high-profile parties, or have influential friends and a fiancé dubbed the next Kennedy? Probably not. That thought made her sad. But it was all the motivation she needed to make sure she cleared her name. Maybe once this was all done Maggie and Mona could sit down together. Maybe not as friends. Certainly not besties. But at least as ladies.

It was the doctor's opinion Mona would survive. But there was a chance she'd have a scar or two.

The attack was quick, not fatal, but brutal, none-theless.

After Gary left Maggie wanted nothing more than to crawl into a hole and sleep until the whole nasty situation blew over. But that was an impossible wish. So, instead of curling up in a fetal position and crying, she pulled herself together and got to work.

## Chapter 15

**D**ust, cobwebs, fingerprints, and footprints disappeared over the course of a couple of hours. Books were removed from their shelves, feather dusted, and placed back in their appropriate places in proper order. In between the cleaning frenzies, Maggie managed a few *hellos*, a handful of *have a nice days*, and one *don't read that book, it's stupid* to an older woman who picked up the latest installment by some hack writer who thought teenage vampires were romantic. By the time she was done, she was sure it had to be almost quitting time. All she wanted was the smokey smell of incense, a strong cup of tea, her soft pajamas, and the doors locked and curtains shut. However, the clock on the wall indicated she had three more hours to go before quitting time.

"Ugh." Maggie sighed. She couldn't let all this get to her. The scandal and rumors and accusations were all false. She knew they were, and anyone who knew her knew they were. But that didn't change the fact that every time someone came into the store and made eye-contact with her Maggie was sure they were part of the ever-widening ring of rumormongers and would be discussing at length her supposed crimes of passion.

After she'd looked at her hands, Maggie realized she should have worn gloves while doing the cleaning. Her hands had become dry and cracked, and a couple of nails had chipped. She wrung them nervously and turned with tired eyes to the door when the chimes jingled. Thank goodness it wasn't a customer. The desire to chitchat, assist, or be friendly in any way had gone out the window.

"Hey, Maggie. How's business been today?" Joshua asked. He was in a good mood. At least one of them was.

"Fine."

Joshua turned around with one eyebrow raised. "Really? That didn't sound fine."

Before he could ask any more questions, Maggie

jerked her thumb toward the canvas-covered display window. "I need a few supplies. Unless you want to… reveal a jacked display."

"Jacked? Well, no. I don't think I want a *jacked* display. You know where the petty cash is. Take what you need," Joshua replied. It was impossible to miss the look of concern on his face. Maggie opened her mouth to tell him what was happening but instead snapped it shut and wrinkled her nose like she was holding back a sneeze. Moving with what felt like the grace of a gazelle when in reality it was more like the poise of a bumper car, Maggie hustled to the office, grabbed some petty cash, squeezed past Joshua, and hurried back to the register to grab her purse from below the counter. Before she knew it, she was outside walking down the sidewalk. The weight on her shoulders caused a fog to settle in her mind.

Everyone else in their cars zooming by on the street and walking past her looked happy and care-free. Like they'd breezed through life and today was going to be blissfully happy without a single shady cloud on the horizon. Yet Maggie, who prided herself on staying quiet and out of the limelight, was not just involved in a murder and an assault but was at the very center of it. How did this happen?

What had she done to upset the applecart of the universe? Part of her wanted to curl up, close her eyes, and wait for justice to prevail. But another part of her, an unfamiliar part, felt like a cat backed into a corner.

In that moment she saw something that she wasn't prepared for. The Fair Haven newspaper. It was a free publication. No one really read it unless they were looking for a used car or an apartment for rent. But there it was on the front page.

"Police Zeroing in on Local Resident in Spencersmith Killing." The byline was Oliver Durham. Maggie snatched a copy from the rack, letting the heavy metal door slam back in place, and began to read. Although it didn't refer to her by name, the description of a female person of interest who was employed at the bookstore in Fair Haven and rented property where the body of Matthew Spencersmith was found was enough to narrow down the suspect list. Of course, Maggie couldn't retaliate because he hadn't called her out by name. Durham was a sneaky one. Maggie folded the paper and tucked it under her arm before she started walking again.

*Have you had enough? When are you going to start fighting back? You've done it for other people. Even put your life in danger. Don't you think it's time you do it for yourself?* her conscience scolded.

Before she realized it she was in front of her favorite thrift store, Sell-It-Again-Sam's. That was a surprise since it didn't feel like she'd walked seven blocks. Her mind had been so preoccupied. But it was a place she enjoyed where she would find enough stuff to not only complete the window display but to also give her mind a rest from its troubles.

As soon as she stepped into the place, her attitude shifted. Some people might not like it, but the smell of mothballs, old books, and leather permeated the building. Instantly, Maggie felt relaxed and calm. Her display needed only a few final touches like colorful scarves or maybe some tacky amateur paintings that were bright and garish. As she walked along looking at anything with bright colors, she barely noticed the man at the counter talking to Sam, the owner. It wasn't until she was almost directly behind him that she recognized his voice.

"She just showed up. What was I supposed to do? She's family," she heard Roger Hawes say in that deep, menacing tone of voice. He was either grumbling like the world had annoyed him permanently or he wasn't speaking at all. Maggie always thought his voice sounded like someone dragging a railroad nail against gravel.

"Sorry to hear that, Roger," Sam replied, glancing at Mr. Hawes before looking down and shaking his head. No one liked to look Roger Hawes in the face for very long. He had a way of conveying disgust and irritation without saying a single word. No one escaped his judgement.

"I know everything happened a long time ago and she's had some great gains at the place she was staying. I just don't think coming back here, where she had all her *trouble*, was a good idea," Mr. Hawes said. "I'm in the middle of acquiring some more property, and I can't have this distraction. Although, she had helped get Spencersmith on board before he was… done in."

Maggie froze behind a tall rack of knickknacks as soon as she heard the name Spencersmith. She peeked around the display, careful to stay out of sight. Roger Hawes was wearing the same drab clothes he always wore, and his imposing stature looked the same from behind as it did from the front. That meant he was scary coming or going.

"That whole story is a little suspicious," Sam replied.

"Did you see the paper today? The authorities

are closing in on someone. It's always the people you least expect. The quiet ones. Especially in small towns like Fair Haven. I hope they throw the book at her," Roger said, an armchair authority on solving crimes.

Maggie had been fired up on the way over reading about herself in the paper even if she wasn't called out by name. Gary saying that Mona singled her out as her attacker was even more infuriating. But to know the town bully was slipping his opinion in was even more exasperating. She clenched her fists and weighed whether she should go set the record straight.

"No. I haven't looked at the paper. So, how long is your niece going to stay?" Sam asked, changing the subject. Maggie let out the breath she hadn't even realized she was holding.

"She's doing a few things for me. I needed a couple shelves fixed in one of my shops, and the girl is handy with tools. Except she lost my hammer. That's a woman for you. So, is this price on these here clock radios the real price, or can we work out a deal?" Roger said without a hint of comedy in his voice. He was dead serious. It wasn't good enough that he found a couple of secondhand radios. He had to shave a few more bucks off the price until he was getting them for practically nothing. Then he'd turn around and sell them at his pawn shop for double.

That was what he tried to do with Mr. Whitfield whenever he came in the bookstore threatening to close it down and take the building from him. That is what he was obviously trying to do to Joshua too. Threatening health inspections and lawsuits was the only way Roger Hawes knew how to do business. He had connections with some people at city hall, at least that was what Maggie had heard. But if it were true, none of those politicians were ever seen actually helping him.

After taking a deep breath and quietly letting it out in an annoyed hiss, Maggie figured she'd get back to the real reason she was at the shop to begin with. There were decorations to buy, and she still had to get back to the bookstore to finish the display. Matthew Spencersmith would still be dead. Mona would still be in the hospital. Nothing was going to change today. However, Maggie suddenly questioned her own health. Was she suddenly seeing a hallucination?

"Uncle Roger! I thought I'd find you here," Colleen called from across the store.

Maggie's mouth went dry as she stared. Her

eyes started to burn. She was afraid to blink. If she did, the whole scene might change. It would prove she was going crazy. Seeing things. If her mind was playing such demented tricks on her that meant there was a possibility she did kill Matthew Spencersmith and beat Mona Plum. No. She had to keep staring no matter what and keep the two figures in focus.

"Hello, Colleen," Roger Hawes muttered. "What have you been up to?"

*She did say uncle, right? I wasn't hearing things. I didn't just dream that, did I?* Maggie thought as she stared.

"A little of this and a little of that," she replied. Maggie blended into the background, slipping even farther into the shadows while watching and listening. With Colleen suddenly appearing, Sam took the opportunity to slip away and avoid changing the prices on the alarm clocks Roger had brought to him.

"Have you had any luck?" Roger asked quietly without looking directly at his niece.

"Look, I'm telling you right now. That bookstore is as good as yours. You might as well start picking out contractors to gut the place," Colleen said. It wasn't even the same person Maggie had been palling around with the night before. This version of Colleen had an oily, slithery nature to her, and any second Maggie expected her to drop to the floor and slither around before coiling up, her forked tongue darting in and out.

"I really wish you'd tell me how you are managing this. But I suppose the less I know the better," Roger replied, barely looking at his niece.

"You'd be surprised what a real estate license and a little persistence can do for a girl," Colleen replied with a smirk that made Maggie's stomach fold over on itself.

"Yeah. But you're sure what you are doing is safe?" Roger's voice was low, guttural, and bordering on angry. "You've been through a lot, and if people find out…"

"Of course. No one is even going to know either one of us had anything to do with anything. It's all on the up-and-up. I promise," Colleen replied.

*What's on the up-and-up?* Maggie wondered whether she should just jump right out and confront the two of them right there or wait.

"Just make sure of that. Without Spencersmith to lobby for me to get that property reevaluated you'll need to talk to some of his constituents. That might be hard for someone new in town," Roger said as he studied the alarm clocks in his hands.

Colleen had a smile plastered on her face, and it had no intention of leaving. It was like watching a gator that at any second was going to notice she was there hiding.

"Being new in town didn't stop Spencersmith. It won't stop anyone else," she said, her lips pouting innocently. Maggie swallowed hard, backed up just a little, and waited. Finally, after what felt like an eternity, Roger Hawes and his niece decided to leave the thrift store. Maggie wanted to run back to the bookshop to warn Joshua, but what exactly would she tell him? Colleen, who she thought was her friend, was actually in cahoots with Roger Hawes to steal the bookshop away from him? It sounded like the plot of some silly book. Still, she had to do something.

*You need to do what you came here for. Nothing gets the brain working like action. Didn't Colleen say that?* she encouraged herself. It was true regardless of who said it. So, with the facts rolling around in the back of her mind, she managed to scoop up exactly what she needed for the window display. As she took her treasures back to the bookstore, she let the sun beat on her face, no longer concerned about the rumors and article in the paper. There was something more sinister going on. Maggie was sure of that. The worst part was that she had been folded into the plans.

But, like Roger had said, in a small town like Fair Haven, it's the quiet ones you have to look out for. Maggie had decided to make a little noise.

# Chapter 16

Wilma DeForrest worked at the Old Cedar Bank. She was the only teller who didn't completely ruffle Maggie's feathers and that was because she rarely spoke to her. Maggie was aware that she gave off a "don't talk to me" vibe, but it seemed Wilma was one of the few who picked up on it. But even Wilma broke her own rule of senseless chitchat with Maggie. Especially since Joshua had come to town. Before, when Maggie worked for Alexander, no one paid much attention to her coming and going with the bank deposit bag. She was as obscure as some of the titles that were on the shelves at the bookshop. But as soon as the extremely handsome and completely eligible bachelor Joshua Whitfield came to town and took over the business, Maggie was suddenly an important bank patron. It annoyed her immensely.

None of the women who worked behind the plexiglass ever had a word to say to her. They'd never set foot in the bookstore. Yet this group of clucking hens was a font of information regarding the happenings in Fair Haven. But now the single ladies at Old Cedar Bank continually bothered Maggie and asked how business at the bookshop was and would Joshua be attending the Christmas gala or the Halloween costume ball or the Fourth of July fireworks. It was all so blatantly obvious what they were up to, Maggie couldn't help but wrinkle her nose in disgust. Not to mention that she didn't think any of them were good enough for Joshua, who wasn't just a pretty face but was kind, dedicated, and darn funny, even if Maggie did bite her tongue at times so he didn't see her laugh.

But today Maggie was determined to handle things differently. If Colleen thought she could swoop into town and start stirring the pot, she might want to be careful where she got her ingredients.

With her heart pounding, blood racing, and a

glint in her eye, Maggie marched up to Wilma's window with all the subtlety of a bulldog in a china shop. It caught the attention of Joyce, one of the bank managers. She was a tall woman who reminded Maggie of an ostrich, as her neck seemed to stretch whenever someone was speaking softly.

"Good morning, Maggie. What can I do for you today?" Wilma asked.

"I need to ask you a couple of questions." Maggie leaned close to the plexiglass partition.

"Okay. Is everything alright?"

"Have you heard Roger Hawes's niece is in town?" Maggie could tell that Wilma had an opinion of Mr. Hawes as soon as she mentioned his name. As if she'd suddenly sucked a lemon, her lips pinched together, and her eyes narrowed. It was only for a split second, but her distaste for the man was unmistakable.

"Does this have to do with bank business?" Wilma asked, finally raising her eyebrows.

"In a way," Maggie lied.

Wilma looked over her shoulder to make sure the coast was clear before she spoke. The other hens were all busy. Maggie had no doubt whatever she said would be discussed at length after she left.

"Yes. Word spread when she was back in town.

She was at that fancy party your landlord had. Did you see her there?"

"I wasn't invited," Maggie said, knowing that tidbit would make it around the bank quicker than a spider up a drainpipe. "Where had she been?"

"You weren't invited? How come?"

Maggie didn't take the bait. She wasn't there to talk about herself. She was on an intel-gathering quest and wasn't going to leave until she knew something more about Colleen.

"Where had she been?" she asked again.

Wilma took another quick glance around. This time, out of the corner of her eye, Maggie could see Joyce taking notice of them chatting. With her breath hitching in her throat, she hoped Wilma would spill something of value.

"You didn't know? She had an episode. They were treating her in New Lenox," Wilma said with her eyebrows raised, her chin down, and her eyes just slits.

Everyone in Fair Haven knew what was in New Lenox. Signs peppered the highway into town warning drivers not to pick up hitchhikers. Every convenience store and gas station had notices in the bathrooms to report any suspicious behavior or individuals to the police immediately. There were a couple hundred acres cut off with a fence adorned with razor wire over the top. It was the shared property of the New Lenox Mental Hospital. At the other end was Stateville Prison. Just a small dirt road separated the two facilities, putting one in Will County and the other in Cook County. As can be imagined, that made for a spiderweb of bureaucratic red tape dealing with the inmates in both places.

"How long was she there?" Maggie asked, trying to hide her surprise by pushing up her glasses and wrinkling her nose.

"I can't say for sure, but I think it was around three or four years. Not everyone is happy she's back in town. I don't even think Roger is all that thrilled," Wilma replied.

Maggie recalled him telling Sam that Colleen had just showed up at his house unannounced. "What did she do?" Maggie's voice was just above a whisper.

"I heard that she—"

"Is everything all right here?" Joyce interrupted. She stood there with her arms folded over her chest and a faker-than-fake bright-red grin on her face.

"Fine." Maggie didn't smile back.

"How is business at the bookstore? Is Joshua settling in for good in Fair Haven? Has he mentioned anyone special lately?" Joyce asked like a hobo peering into a fine restaurant and staring at the people as they ate. Maggie was sure the woman's mouth was watering.

"Business is good," Maggie snapped. Without any paperwork or money to change hands and just her bag of goodies from the thrift store, she tugged at her sleeves and gave a crooked smile to Wilma before turning and stomping out of the bank. It wasn't a complete loss.

"Oh, that Joyce," she muttered as she marched down the sidewalk. "She couldn't just mind her own business for a few more minutes. Just a couple of seconds and I would have known what Colleen was at the mental facility for. Just my luck. I wonder if…"

The idea just came to her. It was so easy. Why hadn't she thought of it before? She had one of the most well-connected individuals at her fingertips and had almost completely forgotten. It was time to pay Mrs. Peacock a visit. This time, Maggie wasn't going to worry about appearing angry. She had every right to be. This whole thing started because of Mrs. Peacock's party.

"She could threaten raising the rent," Maggie mumbled to herself as she made her way back to the bookshop and immediately got to work on the window display. Much to her surprise a couple of young girls came into the store and pointed to Maggie as she bustled about, talking to herself, shaking her head, and waving her hands like there were bees buzzing around her. But Maggie didn't care.

Even when Joshua came from the back storeroom and inspected her display, she didn't care that he stood there with his mouth hanging open in shock at the beautiful scene in front of him.

"Maggie. This is your most beautiful display yet. How... I'm amazed," he said.

Intentionally, Maggie brushed off his praise and asked to leave a couple minutes early. Had she caught his eye she might have forgotten herself and her plans and become that awkward woman who admired her boss from afar never daring to let him know she cared for him.

"Sure. You can leave early. Is everything okay?" he asked.

"Yeah. Why wouldn't everything be okay?" she snapped back.

"I was just asking. You're just really reliable and rarely ask to leave, so I was just—"

"Being nosey?"

"Hey, you're my best employee. I can be concerned if I want to be." Joshua smirked.

"What? Are you afraid I'm going to a job interview somewhere else? You think one of the stores on Main Street is looking to hire a quirky, introverted bookworm to make the rest of the staff feel uncomfortable?"

"You're making *me* uncomfortable." Joshua grinned as he took a slight step forward. With his hands on his hips, he leaned toward Maggie. It was obvious that he wasn't at all intimidated by her, and had Maggie not been in a fight to clear her good name, she would have stayed in that place in the middle of the bookstore forever if it meant seeing Joshua like this. Playful and handsome and knowing that he had her number but also knowing she was too prideful to acknowledge it. She felt the curl start at the corners of her lips and realized it had been days, maybe longer, since she'd actually cracked a smile. She didn't stop it. She smiled wide, and it felt good. Then she wrinkled her nose, shook her head, looked down, and smoothed out her slacks.

"Good," she replied then slowly walked to the counter, grabbed her purse, and walked out of the bookshop. Regardless of what Mrs. Peacock had to say, Maggie thought the day had suddenly turned for the better.

# Chapter 17

Maggie found her landlord in a colorful muumuu relaxing on her massive back patio with a cup of tea, jazzy music playing softly, and a book in her lap. No outfit of Mrs. Peacock's would be complete without the myriad of sparkling gems set in gold on her fingers. It was one of the few times the woman wasn't bustling around fretting over the imaginary wolf just outside her three-inch-thick oak and beveled-glass front door. Right now, at this moment, Maggie was observing a woman without a care in the world.

"Mrs. Peacock?" Maggie called as she made her way up the stone path that wound partially through her garden.

The older woman jumped. "Hello, Maggie. You

surprised me. The rent isn't due for another week. Are you—"

"I need to speak with you. It's important," Maggie said as she made her way to the patio. She was a little out of breath and wished she would have had time to clean up, maybe take a shower and put on a fresh blouse. Mrs. Peacock was always a little intimidating, as she looked like someone who'd stepped off a photoshoot for wealthy widows.

"I do hope the rent won't be late. I'm on a fixed income, and your rent helps me keep my head just above water. I'm barely making it as it is. In fact, there is a very good chance I may have to raise…" She began to ramble.

Maggie was in no mood to hear her woes and started to shake her head before sitting down on the edge of the lawn chair just across the glass coffee table from Mrs. Peacock. "Have I ever been late with my rent?" Maggie snapped.

Mrs. Peacock's mouth hung open for a split second, her eyes wide in surprise.

"No. Mrs. Peacock, I need to ask you something important." Maggie rocked slightly and folded her arms across her belly as if she needed to protect herself from her older landlord who might suddenly give her a jab to the gut.

"Of course, dear. What is it?"

Maggie took a deep breath. As much as Mrs. Peacock annoyed her with her constant whining about finances, she really thought her landlord was a decent person and very lovely. Perhaps it was as simple as Mrs. Peacock didn't think before she spoke. Maybe her social status kept her from realizing how condescending she sounded at times. Perhaps she was lonely for her husband and didn't want to become too attached to anyone for fear of experiencing that loss again. Maggie didn't know. But she knew she had to lay down the law and speak clearly, precisely, and forcefully.

"What do you know about Roger Hawes's niece, Colleen?"

Mrs. Peacock looked like she'd been slapped across the face with a dead fish. After a few seconds of staring with her mouth hanging open, she smoothed out the material of her muumuu, pinched her lips together before licking them, and blinked.

"Colleen Hawes. I was hoping that whole mess would just blow over," she said. "Why are you asking?"

"Does it matter?"

Mrs. Peacock took a deep breath, inspected her

rings, then settled into her seat after closing her book and setting it on the coffee table. "It was a long time ago. She's not the same girl she was when it happened."

"What was a long time ago? What happened?" Maggie pressed.

"When she showed up in town, I didn't even know who she was, exactly. I'd heard she had changed and that she was just keeping to herself. When she showed up at my house with Edmond Donner, I wasn't even sure who I was looking at," Mrs. Peacock replied. "Here was this woman in a slinky dress with one of my guests. What was I going to say? Sorry, dear, but I can't let you in because there are knives on the buffet table?"

Knives? Maggie's heart jumped. What had she gotten herself into? What was Colleen capable of? The woman whose house she'd been in and who she had driven around and confided in was turning out to be a ticking time bomb.

"You said it was a long time ago. What was a long time ago?" Maggie asked.

"When Colleen Hawes's father died," Mrs. Peacock said sadly.

Maggie was sure that her heart had stopped for a couple of seconds. Did this woman kill her own father? How could she be out walking around? She should be in jail. For life. It must have been apparent to Mrs. Peacock what Maggie was thinking because she quickly shook her head and extended her arm to pat the air in a reassuring manner.

"No. It's not what you think. Colleen and her father were very close. He was a contractor. She got into real estate. He drove an expensive pickup truck. She had to have one too. She was a daddy's girl, and he was her hero. The one habit he had that Colleen never picked up was smoking. When he got the diagnosis of stage four cancer..." Mrs. Peacock stopped and looked out at her garden. Maggie leaned closer.

"Some people are not mentally equipped to handle an unexpected tragedy. Colleen Hawes is one of those people."

Maggie felt a pit form in her stomach. She heard Roger Hawes talking with his niece about the bookstore and taking it from Joshua. How could a woman be so sensitive in one area and be so cruel in another?

"What did she do?" Maggie asked.

"She blamed the doctors for her father dying. There were two men that she interacted with. One was the specialist. I believe his name was Alberts." Mrs. Peacock tapped her chin as she focused on the coffee table before meeting Maggie's eyes. "But it was Doctor Lenny Cameron that she focused her rage on. The poor man nearly died."

"How?"

"It started like so many sad cases like this do. Colleen put all her faith in Dr. Cameron, and no matter how hard he tried to tell her to prepare for the worst, she wouldn't listen. When her father finally succumbed to his illness, Colleen filed a lawsuit. Of course, it was tossed out. She started stalking Dr. Cameron. There were phone calls. Eventually she showed up at his office. This went on for weeks. Then she found out where he lived. One night she decided if her father couldn't be alive, the man who sentenced him to death shouldn't be either."

Maggie leaned back and put her hand to her throat.

"She broke into his house with a mallet. After a tussle she managed to get in a couple of good licks, but Dr. Cameron had a security system. The police were on their way the minute she'd broken the window to get in."

"Why isn't she still in jail?" Maggie asked.

"Doesn't attempted murder get a person sent away for a long time?"

"She never went to jail." Mrs. Peacock looked down her nose as if she were doing nothing more than explaining a simple math problem.

"What?"

Again Mrs. Peacock studied her rings and smoothed out the fabric of her muumuu over her lap. "It was decided that she was not mentally fit to stand trial. It was decided that her mental ability to understand what she'd done was not there. In a nutshell, the death of her father drove her insane. So she went to New Lenox for treatment."

Maggie took a deep breath. Part of her felt sorry for Colleen. To have a loved one die unexpectedly of a disease had to be a pain Maggie could never understand without experiencing it herself. It was hard enough when Mr. Whitfield had died of natural causes because he was an old man. He was not her father, no matter how fatherly he acted. But she still missed him. It was not hard to understand the feeling of loneliness and even abandonment. Sometimes shadows take up residence, even with the sun shining and all the lights on.

"Once the court had Colleen institutionalized, Dr. Cameron recovered from his injuries but left town. He was not going to take the chance of her getting out and trying to finish the job she started. I don't know where he ended up." Mrs. Peacock pinched her lips together sadly.

"Did the people at New Lenox help her?" Maggie had been in close quarters with Colleen and had an uneasy feeling about their friendship since learning she was a mental patient. It's one thing if she had bouts of depression. But an uncontrollable rage triggered by things out of anyone's control? That was different.

"There wasn't much they could do. As it turned out, this was not the first person she'd blamed for her issues. She'd stalked and threatened a professor at her college for a grade she thought was unfair. There had been two fiancés who also suffered her tantrums before dodging the bullet, as they say." Mrs. Peacock raised her chin but looked to her left as if she had just noticed the giant planters with rubber trees growing in them.

"Two fiancés?" Maggie muttered. She'd never gotten anywhere near going steady with a fella, let alone two engagements.

"As far as I know, there is no cure for narcissism."

Maggie swallowed, but her mouth was dry. This

couldn't change anything. A sob story was just that. A story. It was the actions that really mattered. Maggie felt that Colleen's actions overshadowed the sympathy for losing her father.

"Why are you asking about this?" Mrs. Peacock asked with one eyebrow arched up high.

"Since your party I've had some trouble with some of the guests. Colleen Hawes was one of them," Maggie replied. It was her turn to look down her nose at Mrs. Peacock.

"What kind of trouble?"

Maggie stood up, smoothed her slacks, and thanked Mrs. Peacock for the information. She took two steps before stopping and turning around.

"It hurt my feelings that you didn't invite me to your party. If I'm that much of an embarrassment, perhaps it's time I look for a new apartment," Maggie stated.

Of course, she didn't want to leave her home. But maybe it was time she had an apartment in a building with other units and neighbors right next door. She heard Mrs. Peacock gasp. Perhaps she was going to say something snide back or maybe just a gasp and then a harumph, and an eviction notice would be taped to Maggie's door the next morning.

"Why, Maggie, I didn't think—"

"I've got to get home. It's getting late," Maggie lied and shuffled down the path to her cottage. If Mrs. Peacock had wanted to continue talking to her, she could have spoken louder. Maggie's front door was just a hop, skip, and jump from the back patio. She would have heard her landlord loud and clear. But as it was just the sound of crickets and the last squeaky chirps of a couple of blue jays before nightfall that she heard, she unlocked her front door and slipped inside.

*Don't worry. Whatever Mrs. Peacock does you'll be able to handle it*, that little voice in her head said confidently. For once, Maggie agreed. Now, what was she going to do with the information she had on Colleen?

## Chapter 18

As Maggie made herself some tea, her mind whirred, processing the new information she had about Colleen. She could hear the rumbling inside the teapot as the water slowly started to boil. With it she felt along the edges of an idea. Maybe slipping up to New Lenox Mental Hospital might yield some fruit. If she was going to try and anticipate this woman's next move, knowing where she spent some serious time might be helpful.

"They won't tell you anything. You're not family," she stated while standing on tiptoes and reaching up into the cabinet over her sink in the kitchen. There she found a vintage tin she'd picked up years ago. Yellow. Faded. With strawberries on the vine weaving all around it. When she popped the top, inside was her stash of teas.

"Maybe just taking a stroll around the grounds. No. That won't work. First, who wouldn't think it a little suspicious if I just showed up there and asked to be given a tour. Second, it is a hospital. The people who are there are sick. No. That won't work." Maggie continued to talk to herself. "Perhaps a late-night surveillance of the place. Maybe just a drive around the neighborhood would give me a sense of what makes Colleen tick."

That idea was quickly shaken loose as a shiver raced across her shoulder blades. People might call her insensitive, but she couldn't help but recall the images of Nurse Ratched and the depressing, sterile environment that lacked any kind of softness portrayed in Ken Kesey's book. A mass of hard edges and flat surfaces with no personal touches.

*No. I doubt mental hospitals are like that anymore,* she thought as she pulled out two peppermint tea bags. She dropped them into the big mug that was always on her stove just as the teapot started to whistle.

"Margaret, you're going to have to do something a lot more intense than going to New Lenox Mental Hospital. You're going to have to face a fear that you might not be prepared to face," she declared as she soaked her tea bags in the steaming hot water. The peppermint smell wove its way up to her nostrils, giving her a sense of calm. She raised the mug to her lips and took a tiny sip. The heat of the water mixed with the cooling sensation of the peppermint refreshed her. She took a seat at her small kitchen table and listened to the quiet. It wasn't scary or unnerving. She was home, in her small cottage, and everything was in its place. The new lock on her door was sturdy. Her windows were all shut. The soft scent of a vanilla candle still lingered even though she hadn't lit it since the night of Mrs. Peacock's party.

"You're going to have to go and talk to Roger Hawes," she said. Hearing her own voice cut through the quiet made her decision all the more real. She didn't like Roger Hawes. She never had. It wasn't just that he was rude and bossy. But Roger had an aura about him that ruffled Maggie's feathers. That air of superiority and condescending tone of voice was bad enough, but the fact he was a large man and could easily intimidate smaller people did nothing but make him more of a Goliath.

"He'll probably be more tight-lipped than the staff at New Lenox," Maggie muttered before taking another sip of her tea. But that wasn't enough to stop her. Maggie was in the center of this because Colleen had put her there. Roger wouldn't be able to deny that he knew his niece was up to something because she'd heard it at the thrift store come out of his own mouth. Something that had to do with the bookstore, and that was just another avenue of Maggie's livelihood that Colleen had focused on messing up.

With renewed vigor, Maggie decided that she would go talk to Roger sooner rather than later. The pawn shop was open until ten o'clock in the evening. It wasn't in the best neighborhood, and as it got later the questionable characters looking to hock a gold watch they found or a ruby ring that had been their late mother's would go up. Maggie didn't care. She was tired of letting them take the lead in this fiasco. She gulped down the rest of her tea, set the cup in the sink, changed from her work clothes into jeans and gym shoes in case she had to run for any reason, grabbed her keys and purse, and headed out the door.

As she drove, she gave herself a pep talk. "Roger Hawes puts his pants on one leg at a time just like everyone else. Just because he's a big man and grumbles all the time and always looks like he's sucked on a raw lemon most of the time doesn't mean he's scary. In fact, it might mean he's as scared of talking to people as you are sometimes, Margaret."

She took a deep breath as she drove, let it out, and rolled her eyes. "Who are you kidding. He's mean. Plain and simple. That's all there is to it."

As she came to a stoplight, she wondered if maybe she shouldn't just turn around and wait to talk to him some other time, if at all. But then she remembered how Colleen had acted and wondered if she was still playing a game with Maggie or had decided the death blow was to be dealt sooner rather than later.

After another deep breath she saw the faded and chipping billboard with the words Roger Hawes Pawn Shop. Below it on the blank wall of the brick building was the same heading with an arrow pointed to the front entrance.

"Nothing to be scared of Maggie. She's not your friend. You aren't going to be threatening anyone. You just need to ask a couple of questions. The worst that could happen is you leave here with nothing. Nothing. Nothing isn't so bad. It's like zero. Just another word for bupkus. Zilch," she babbled as she pulled into the potholed parking lot trying not to pop a tire as she maneuvered her way around. She saw there were cameras outside the place. The windows had bars across them, and the displays of fine jewelry and watches looked like a grandmother's old-fashioned jewelry box had exploded across the shag carpet. Had Mr. Hawes been a decent man, Maggie would have been happy to redo his display. But, at the moment, she wasn't sure she wanted to share the same zip code with him.

"Okay. Let's get this over with," Maggie said as she put her car in park, shut it off, and opened her car door. It didn't smell good in this part of town. It was a mixture of car exhaust and greasy fries from the string of fast-food joints down the street. Maggie looked up at the cameras as she walked to the front door. She yanked the glass door, but it held fast. Then, the sound of a buzzer coming from inside and a lock's clack indicated the door had been unlocked.

A hulking man with coffee-colored skin sat on a stool and smiled politely. "What can I help you with tonight?"

"I need to speak to the owner," Maggie replied, hoping the security guard didn't detect the waves of nervousness in her voice. The man said nothing more but nodded in the direction of a long glass case. Behind it was a closed door.

Maggie wasn't sure if she should walk behind the counter and knock or if someone would come out on their own or what. She waited a couple of seconds, taking in the inventory of the Roger Hawes Pawn Shop.

The first thing Maggie noticed was that the place could use a thorough airing out. There was a musty smell like there might have been flooding or a leak in the ceiling during a torrential rainfall that caused half the place to get drenched. Instead of tearing up the carpet and paneling they just propped up a couple of box fans and let the place dry out over the course of a week or two.

Second, there was not just gold jewelry and pocket watches being pawned. There were tools that looked like they came straight from a showroom floor. Musical instruments were dinged and dented but still able to produce a halfway decent sound. Off to the right was a bin full of audio cassette tapes and DVDs. To the left were small appliances like coffeemakers and blenders. Maggie was sure she saw the alarm clocks Roger had been haggling over with Sam at the thrift store. They had price tags dangling from them. Maggie walked up, turned one of the tags, and rolled her eyes. A plain, no-nonsense digital clock without the original box or instructions was not worth twenty dollars. How did he ever turn a profit?

Then she spotted something that was completely out of place but sent a shiver up her spine. In the farthest corner, stacked like kindling, were books. Not just any books but a vast array of old books, some pulp, some classics, all in sad shape as they were under a layer of dust and, Maggie was sure, rife with silverfish. When she walked over, she got a strange feeling that this was where a couple of books had been taken from that found their way to her. She couldn't prove it, but she knew only one of the books had The Bookish Café stamped on the inside.

Maggie put her hands on her hips and thought about rescuing a couple of titles until she picked one up and looked at the price.

"Ten dollars for *The Catcher in the Rye*?" she turned the book over in her hand. "It's a mass production version and like a thirtieth printing. It's not worth more than the cover price of $1.99." Maggie rolled her eyes. She looked at the security guard as if he would understand. He watched her casually with no expression on his face. Maggie let out an annoyed chuckle and put the book back.

Just then the door behind the glass counter opened. Before Maggie took two steps, Roger Hawes appeared, looking like he had just been hoping someone would mess with him. But the way his body jerked slightly when he saw her gave Maggie a feeling of satisfaction that her presence was not just a surprise but an unpleasant one.

"Mr. Hawes. I need to speak to you," Maggie said. She was sure he could see her knees suddenly start shaking, but she lifted her chin and stared up the nine inches to his doughy face without blinking.

"Okay. What about?" he barked. The man had the manners of a junkyard dog.

Maggie cleared her throat. "About your niece, Colleen."

"What about her?"

"I want to know if you think she should be out of New Lenox or did the doctors there make a mistake." Maggie rattled the words off quickly so they wouldn't get tied up by her tongue.

The color drained from Roger's face. "What are you talking about?"

"I also want to know what Spencersmith had to

do with reevaluating the bookstore." She shifted from one foot to the other as she squinted at him.

"I don't know what you are talking about. I think you better leave my store," Roger grumbled, but Maggie noticed one thing that gave her a little bump of courage. Roger Hawes quickly looked to the left then proceeded to avoid eye contact with her. In a book she'd read on body language, looking to the left was usually a sign of deception. Roger was trying not to let Maggie know he knew exactly what she was talking about.

"Did she have anything to do with the fire in the alley?"

"What? No. Of course not," he snapped back.

"I saw her at Mrs. Peacock's party with Matthew Spencersmith and Mona Plum. She wanted to break into my cottage. Any idea why a grown woman would want to do such a thing? Why would she encourage a young up-and-coming politician type to do that? I heard it with my own ears." Maggie pouted her lips.

"Logan, if this woman isn't going to buy anything, I think you might need to show her to her vehicle." Roger tried to act casual, but Maggie noticed one thing. He was nervously jingling the change or his keys in his pants pocket.

"It's all right, Logan. I'll see myself out," Maggie said, putting her hand up and taking a step toward the door. "Anything you'd like me to tell Joshua before I go? Anything about politicians reevaluating his property that he owns? Anything?"

The muscles along Roger's jawline tightened, but he said nothing before turning and going back behind the door he'd emerged from. It shut with a solid thud.

"Ma'am," Logan said. Maggie put her hands up and walked to the door. Once she was outside, she took a deep breath of the greasy, exhaust-filled air and felt her shoulders sink down. Her muscles had been so tense and strained, but she hadn't noticed until she was able to relax. When she sat down in her car, it was like sitting in one of those massage chairs at the mall.

Sure, she hadn't conquered Mount Everest or swum a coral reef. But she took a stand against someone bigger than her. Maybe she didn't do anything more than annoy Roger Hawes. But that was a start. Maggie Bell was not going to be intimidated by him anymore.

But then, as if her night couldn't get any better, just as she turned the key and started her car, she saw a very annoyed and red-faced Roger Hawes burst out of the back door of the pawn shop, stomp to his old truck, squeeze himself behind the wheel, and before she could say

damage control, peel out of the parking lot, unaware she was still there watching.

Maggie looked at the clock on her dashboard. "It's still early. May as well go for a drive," she mused as she threw the car into gear and drove off in pursuit.

## Chapter 19

The sun was setting as Maggie followed Roger Hawes from his pawn shop. For all she knew he was going home because he suddenly remembered he left his iron on or a cake in the oven. Of course, based on his appearance she was sure he didn't actually leave an iron on. It was a safe bet he didn't own one. As for the cake, he probably wished he had one in the oven as his waist was not svelte in the least. But Maggie didn't peg him as a baker or cook of any kind. Frozen dinners and tubs of ice cream were the closest he came to home cooking.

Still, he was pushing sixty-five miles an hour in a fifty-mile-an-hour zone. Maggie kept pace with his car as she wondered why he was breaking the speed limit while simultaneously hoping there were no speed traps along the route.

About half an hour out of Fair Haven, Roger Hawes took an exit, made a left, then a right, and then another right before pulling down a quiet street and parking. Quickly, Maggie swerved toward the curb and parked her car, cutting the engine immediately. Within seconds he was out of his truck and hustling as fast as his bulky body would move to the front door of a sprawling ranch house. At first, Maggie thought it was a motel, as there were four additional doors with numbers on them. But it was an odd place for a motel.

Maggie got out of her car, and as the shadows started to creep over the street and sidewalk, she inched her way closer to get a better look. Birds chirped overhead, and the swoosh of traffic a couple streets over could be heard along with a lawnmower somewhere in the distance. Then, she heard Roger.

"Well, where is she? She's supposed to be here! I know you people are getting paid a lot of money to make sure she follows the rules, and..."

The softer voice of a female could be heard but only as a muttering. Maggie couldn't make out what she was saying. Carefully she crept a little closer. A large oak in the front yard had obstructed the view of a sign that read Cretemonee Sober Living Home. When Maggie saw that she tilted her head to the right. A sober living home? Who lived here? Who was Roger looking for? Whoever it was obviously wasn't there, and Roger had a string of obscenities at the ready before stomping off to his truck, revving the engine loudly, and peeling out, making the tires squeal. Maggie crouched in the shadows along the street like she had at Mona's house.

"If this ends with someone else getting beat up and it gets pinned on me, I'm going to pack my things and leave Fair Haven to join the French Foreign Legion," she murmured as she stood from her hiding place. Curiosity had taken hold and was not going to let go.

Like she was walking a tightrope, Maggie crept along the sidewalk and up a narrow slab stone path to the front porch of the building. Had the sign not been there, Maggie would have thought it was a bed-and-breakfast or maybe an antiques shop. The kind that was in a sprawling house but on the inside was a bunch of small rooms and crannies stuffed with old-fashioned doodads and bric-a-brac.

There was a white swing on the east side of the

porch and two rocking chairs on the west side. There were three standing ashtrays with dozens of butts in each.

"He was looking for her again," Maggie heard through the screen door. "I don't know how many times I have to tell that man that his niece wasn't here. I don't know where she is, but I'm worried about her."

"Lindsey, you know this is how it goes sometimes. They have to want to help themselves," a soft-spoken man replied.

"But she was different."

"Just because Colleen wasn't an addict in the same way we are used to doesn't mean she's not addicted to the feeling she gets doing the things she does. To be honest, I wish she was like our other guests because at least we know what we are dealing with," the man said.

Maggie couldn't stand it any longer. She had to find out more. Before she had time to overthink the situation or let fear overcome her, she knocked on the screen's doorframe.

"Can I help you?" It was the same soft, female voice Maggie had heard in mumbles just a few minutes before. She'd expected to see a thin, frail woman in an apron with her hair pulled back in a bun. Instead, she was greeted by a blond bob and shoulders like a linebacker's. Her face was soft, and her eyes were full of interest.

Maggie introduced herself and made the admission that she knew Mr. Hawes and his niece and just wanted to ask a couple questions.

"I understand you might not want to tell me certain things," Maggie said as she squinted at the woman. "But I feel I have to ask anyways."

The woman looked over her shoulder at the other person she'd been talking to and must have gotten the okay sign, as she pushed the screen door open for Maggie to come in. Lindsey motioned for Maggie to take a seat in what was a parlor designed for visitors who weren't staying long. The seats were hard and uncomfortable. The pictures on the wall were drab and uninteresting.

"Welcome to Cretemonee Sober Living Home. My name is Lindsey Cunningham. I'm sort of like the housemother, if you will." She smiled. "This is Ray Mooey. He's our maintenance man."

"Jack of all trades, master of none." Ray extended his hand to Maggie, who accepted as she smiled awkwardly.

"What can we do for you, Maggie?" Lindsey

said as she sat on the arm of the sofa and motioned for Maggie to sit.

After choosing a stiff-backed armchair, Maggie sat on the very edge, tugged at her sleeves, and took a deep breath before beginning. Without coming right out and accusing Colleen of being a complete sociopath, Maggie tiptoed through the facts she knew so far and gave them to Lindsey and Ray like a peace offering.

"I met Colleen officially at the bookstore I work at," Maggie said. "But I first encountered her at the party on my landlord's property. Mrs. Vivian Peacock." She stopped, hoping the name-dropping might prove helpful. They just stared, waiting for Maggie to continue. So, she did—with a bang, mentioning Colleen's behavior, her comments, and her desire to break into her cottage with Spencersmith before his fiancée put the kibosh on that idea. "That was also where Matthew Spencersmith's body was found. He was murdered. You knew about that, right?"

Lindsey looked at Ray before speaking. "You don't think Colleen had anything to do with this man being killed, do you?"

"I don't know." Maggie shrugged.

"Because we were under the impression that she

had been getting help for debilitating depression and suicidal tendencies. That was why we agreed to house her here. There is always someone around. We have rules. We wanted to help," Lindsey said.

"Look. This is a sober living house. This isn't a place for parolees to list as their home address when they report to their probation officers. We only took Colleen in because—" Ray started to explain before Lindsey cleared her throat.

"Because?" Maggie asked, her eyebrows meeting her hairline.

"I know her uncle. He helped smooth out a few rough patches when we were first getting the home started. He knew a lot of people in town, and when you want to have a place like this in a neighborhood where there are children, some folks disagree," Lindsey replied.

If Maggie had to guess, she was sure that Roger's involvement was greasing a few palms and convincing a couple of city inspectors to look the other way instead of at a couple minor infractions. Maggie was starting to see a pattern in the crotchety old pawn shop owner's behavior. It wasn't what he knew but *who*. No wonder losing track of Colleen had him so angry.

"I see," Maggie said and stiffened in her seat.

She was sure her tone of voice sounded like she was recording the conversation for *60 Minutes*. Suspicious and stuffy.

"We've done nothing illegal. In fact, Colleen isn't even staying here. So, if there are any problems, we are——" Lindsey started but Maggie shook her head.

"Did she ever stay here?" Maggie asked.

Lindsey looked at Ray, who chimed in. "No. She was supposed to stay here after she was released from New Lenox. Her uncle arranged it. She'd been away for several years. Mr. Hawes said she'd come to terms with her issues and was ready to start her life over. We love to hear that sort of thing."

"That's true. We want anyone who comes through our door to succeed. We tell them they are welcome but hope they never have to come back. Except for a friendly visit." Lindsey chuckled. "This was a much better place than the flop house they usually sent the female patients to upon release. But she never showed up."

"And she obviously hadn't told her uncle she decided not to stay here either." Ray shrugged.

Maggie felt a chill prick its way across her shoulder blades. If Colleen was supposed to have housing here at the Cretemonee Sober Living

House, then how did she manage to get a house to live in closer to town? She said she was renting it, but she obviously just got out of the facility, so how could she afford it? Her uncle wasn't paying for it or else he wouldn't have come here looking for her. Whose house was she living in? Where was the owner?

*You're freaking out, Mags. Calm down. Maybe she's wealthy? Maybe she saved and invested wisely and has the funds to rent a house on her own.* Her thoughts raced as she recalled being alone in the sparsely decorated home with a person who had the tendency to be violent. Extremely violent.

"Miss Bell? Are you all right?" Lindsey interrupted Maggie, startling her out of her thoughts.

"I've got to go. Thank you for your time." Maggie stood up abruptly and took a step toward the door.

"Wait. Miss Bell. You look like you've seen a ghost. Let me get you a glass of water." Lindsey stood, but Maggie put her hands up and wrinkled her nose.

"No. I'm okay." She squared her shoulders and lifted her chin, finding her manners like a safety pin at the bottom of her purse. She extended her hand to Lindsey and Ray, giving them as best a smile she could. It made her look slightly gassy as she thanked them for their time and invited them to come to the bookstore.

Without hesitating a second longer she left through the front screen door. The crickets were out chirping. The streetlights were on, casting an eerie circle every couple of feet down the street. Traffic had eased on the street, but a few blocks over where it was busier the sound of buses pulling away from the curbs and a couple of honking horns floated over the trees.

The patter of Maggie's footsteps along the lonely sidewalk bounced back to her, making it sound like there was another set. Nervously, she kept looking over her shoulder, half expecting Colleen to be catching up to her with a wide, crazy grin like Norman Bates at the end of the movie *Psycho*. When she was finally behind the wheel of her car, she let out a sigh of relief after locking the doors and making sure there was no one in the backseat.

With it being nighttime now and there no longer being a truck she had to keep up with, Maggie drove back home at a regular pace. She put on the radio but barely heard the songs. Churning over and over in her mind were all the facts she knew so far. For some reason, Maggie was convinced Colleen was a real head case. But was she as dangerous as everyone said?

It was like pulling a rubber band to the point just before it broke. If nothing else, Colleen had lied about who she really was. Sure, it would have been difficult at first to deal with the sideways looks and whispers from people after coming back from New Lenox. But no one ever died of embarrassment. Maggie might not have talked to her immediately, but being the fodder for her own scandals, Maggie knew that things did blow over. People moved on and usually weren't as interested in you as you thought they were. She would have talked to Colleen person-to-person just because she liked books.

But not to tell her that she was Roger Hawes's niece and play along like they were really going to be friends so she could manipulate Maggie, that was dirty. Not to mention what they planned on doing with the bookstore. How many people would they hurt to get what they wanted? Maggie gripped the steering wheel until her knuckles were white.

When she finally reached home, she yawned before turning off the lights and the ignition and getting out of her car. It was at that precise moment when she slammed the car door that she noticed the damage. The window to the tiny workshop on the northern side of the house had been smashed.

She pulled out her keys and unlocked the back door to inspect the damage. That was where she found it. The book *Death Becomes Her* tied to a brick had been tossed through the window. Maggie didn't touch anything. Slowly she backed out of the little room, careful not to bump into any of the empty flowerpots or lawn displays. This was too much. Maggie clenched her jaw and fists and decided she needed help.

Once inside her house she dialed the number she knew by heart.

"This is Officer Brookes," Gary barked into the phone.

"It's Maggie. I didn't want to call 911."

"Are you all right?"

"I don't think so. Someone threw a book tied to a brick through my workshop window," Maggie said.

"A book?"

"Tied to a brick. I think I know who did it."

"What was the book?" Gary asked.

"I just told you I think I know who did it."

"And I heard you. I'm just curious."

"Curious about the title of the book more than the name of the person who did it? Gary... I don't even... are you serious?" Maggie shook her head. Surprisingly, she wasn't as shaken up by the whole situation as she expected. She was angry more than anything else. The vandal didn't realize that now she was going to have to tell Mrs. Peacock and get a lecture about how much it will cost to replace the window. Not to mention she'd threatened her landlord with moving out already. This would probably speed up the process. Something Maggie wasn't prepared for. Why did she have to threaten to leave? She let her temper get the best of her. She didn't even know she had a temper. She knew she had a last nerve that most people got on. But that usually resulted in nothing more than a couple of sarcastic remarks and a look of disgust.

"To be honest, I already have a good idea of who you are going to say. The niece of a certain pawn shop owner," Gary replied as he stood from his desk. "I'll be at your place in a few minutes. Lock your door, and don't open for anyone but me. Got it? Just me."

Maggie nodded even though Gary couldn't see it. "*Death Becomes Her*," she said as she studied the book tied to the rock.

# Chapter 20

By the time Gary showed up, Maggie was a tornado of emotions. On one hand she was terrified that her house had been vandalized. But in the same breath she was beyond angry at the audacity of the vandal. She was scared of telling Mrs. Peacock about the incident but also felt it served her right, as some of the blame Maggie delegated to her landlord. Rightly or wrongly, Mrs. Peacock did have Colleen at her home.

"So where did you say Colleen said she was staying?" Gary asked as he sat again in her kitchen, taking up most of the room with his broad shoulders and clunky utility belt.

"I was there." Maggie described the bungalow

and gave him the address. "I didn't realize she was off her rocker. Maybe I shouldn't say it that way, but the girl isn't all there." Maggie pointed to her temple.

"I know where that is. I'm going to go and check it out," Gary said, looking at his watch. "I'll be officially off duty by the time I get there. Maybe I should—"

"We're going to check it out," Maggie said and grabbed a sweater from the back of her kitchen chair.

"*We* aren't going to do anything. I'm going, and that's final," Gary said before standing up and slipping his notebook back in his breast pocket.

"Gary, she's after me. For all I know she's still skulking around Mrs. Peacock's garden waiting for you to leave. She did throw a rock in my window with a threat tied to it. You can't seriously leave me behind." Maggie looked up at him with her hands on her hips.

It wasn't often that Gary Brookes bent the rules, but he was worried about Maggie being left alone. If she was right and someone was waiting in the shadows for him to leave so they could treat her like they did Matthew Spencersmith, he'd never be able to forgive himself. Besides, he was almost off duty.

There was nothing in the rule book about taking a witness to verify a location after hours. In the middle of the night.

"All right. You can come. But, Margaret Bell, if you try to overstep your bounds, I'll handcuff you, stuff you in the back of the squad car, and then write you a seventy-five-dollar ticket for disobeying an officer of the peace. Capiche?"

"Yes. I understand." Maggie moped.

Before she could think of anything to say in her own defense, they were on the road. Maggie made a couple of attempts to speak but ended up changing her mind, snapping her mouth shut each time. Gary appeared not to notice as he concentrated on driving. There was practically no one on the street at this hour. The entire day had slipped by like she'd been watching it on a screen. So much had happened, and yet she felt there was still nothing to pin on Colleen except being weird. The miles skipped past in the dark only marked by red, yellow, and green traffic lights or porch lights of soft amber. Anything could be taking place around her, and Maggie would know nothing about it. It was exciting being out at night like this when the world was getting ready to turn in for the night.

"So, how are things at the bookstore?" Gary asked, startling Maggie out of her thoughts.

"Good," she replied, wrinkling her nose. "Why? What have you heard?"

Gary chuckled. "I haven't heard anything. I was just asking. You're happy there? The boss, Joshua, he's treating you okay?"

Maggie nodded, her curls bouncing. The humidity in the evening air had tightened them up. She waited to see if Gary was going to say anything else. Suddenly Mrs. Peacock's words about Gary came back to her, and a sweat broke out under her arms.

"I have eyes, Margaret," Mrs. Peacock had said regarding how Gary looked at her. What was she talking about? They had been friends since high school. That was it. There was never anything romantic between the two of them. Besides, Gary knew too much about her. He knew how shy she usually was and how much she hated crowds and being in social settings. During their teen years it wasn't uncommon for Gary to sit with her while she read a book and he did homework that should have been done earlier. Sometimes not a word would pass between the two of them for over an hour, yet there was nothing uncomfortable about it.

"What about you?"

"What about me?" Gary asked as they made a right turn.

"Everything good with you?"

"Yeah. Everything is good," he replied.

"Good." Maggie nodded.

"Mags?"

"Yeah?"

"What's on your mind?"

Maggie rolled her eyes. "Well, I've just had a rock with a threat thrown through the window of my rented home by a woman I thought was my friend who is actually a couple of fries short of a Happy Meal and I come to find out she's supposed to be in a recovery home... recovering... but instead she's at a house that isn't hers and is quite possibly responsible for the murder of a guy found in my yard and... I was in her house... that really isn't her house... alone... without anyone knowing..." She let out a deep breath. "I think Colleen Hawes is dangerous, and I'm a little freaked out. I didn't do anything to her. Or to Mona Plum. You know me, Gary. Probably better than anyone. How did all this end up in my lap?"

Gary looked both ways at a stop sign before driving through. "I think you were in the wrong place at the wrong time. Plus, I don't think Colleen or Mona know who they are dealing with. You might not be the biggest dog in the fight, but you've got the biggest fight out of all the dogs."

"You're calling me a dog, Gary."

"The fiercest dog in the dog park, Mags."

She had to chuckle and looked at her friend, who was smirking proudly at his own comment.

"So, what are we going to do when we get to the house?" Maggie asked, feeling free to discuss the situation with Gary like the old friends they were.

"You are going to wait in the car. I'm going to park down the street and take a walk. You're sure you know which house it is?"

"Yup," Maggie replied. It was the only bungalow on the block. The decor was simple. "What do you mean I'm going to wait in the car?"

"Exactly that. There is something strange about her being in this house. I'm not going to go in. I'm going to try knocking on the door. I can't very well have you with me when I do. How would that look? It's bad enough I'm taking you on this impromptu ride-along. So, you are staying put."

Maggie folded her arms, twisted her mouth, then nodded.

"I'm afraid I know which house you are talking

about. Is it that one?" Gary pointed to the bungalow Maggie had gone inside.

"How did you know?"

"It's been for sale for over a year. The owners live in Florida. Can't seem to unload it for whatever reason. The Realtor is friends with Gloria. Stops in all the time asking me when I'm gonna move out of my apartment into a house." Gary's eyebrows rose slightly higher to indicate his annoyance.

"You don't want to own a house someday?"

"Not this one," Gary said as he parallel parked on the next block. "Sit tight. I won't be long. I'm just going to take a quick look around."

Maggie did as she was told and nestled into the leather front seat while keeping an eye out for anyone who might look like Colleen. The last thing she wanted was for Gary to be in any trouble. Even if he was wearing his uniform and badge and side holster, they were dealing with an unpredictable person. Maggie went over the details of the night she was in that little bungalow house. She'd squeezed into the garage between the wall and Colleen's car. There was nothing that could have stopped Colleen from closing and locking the garage door while Maggie was in the bathroom. She had ample opportunity to corner her when she came out of the bathroom too. Plus, there was nothing to stop Colleen from clobbering Maggie over the head with any one of the tools in the back-seat of her car.

Suddenly, it wasn't clear to her if the tempera-ture outside had suddenly dropped or if Maggie's blood had just turned to ice. The hammer sticking out of the toolbox might have been the hammer Gary was looking for. He'd said the one they found in the yard with her own fingerprints on it didn't match the injuries on the body. Could it be that the weapon used to kill Matthew Spencersmith was sitting in the backseat of Colleen's Audi?

Maggie's heart started to race. What should she do? Should she get out of the car and go tell Gary? What if he was at the front door talking to Colleen, asking her some questions, and she ruined the whole surprise attack? But what if he decided to sneak around the back of the house and she heard him? What if he tripped and twisted an ankle just as he was trying to get away from her?

"Oh, Margaret. Calm down," she scolded. "Gary knows what he's doing. He's trained to do these kinds of things. To investigate. That's his job."

Still, with this knew revelation that Colleen could be in possession of a murder weapon, Maggie couldn't contain the urge to get out of the car and warn Gary. He didn't know about the tools in the car.

"If Colleen catches him snooping around, she won't be in the wrong to take action. Even if she knew he was a policeman, all she has to say is someone was skulking around her house at night. She couldn't see who it was and was just defending herself." Maggie was talking herself into ignoring what Gary had said about staying put. What if something happened to him? She'd never be able to forgive herself. Better to take action and deal with the consequences later. Carefully, she pulled the door handle, and the latch gave a loud *chonk* as the passenger-side door opened.

It was only a matter of seconds before she was in front of Colleen's house. There was no sign of Gary. Maggie waited a few minutes and paced a little as she chewed her thumbnail.

"I seem to be doing a lot of suspicious loitering in front of houses these days," she muttered. The thought of the people of Fair Haven associating her with even weirder behavior than she already displayed made her shake her head and frown in disgust. She pulled up her courage from the tips of her toes and marched up the driveway. With no sign of Gary in the front, she quickly walked around the side of the house.

Light came from a neighbor's back porch. The backyard was devoid of any decorations, and the grass was a little longer than the front. As Maggie squinted through the darkness, letting her eyes adjust, she saw a For Sale sign propped behind what Maggie knew was a lilac bush. For a moment the smell brought a sense of relaxation. But then what Gary had said about this place being for sale sunk in. No one was supposed to be living here.

It was an unnerving sensation for Maggie to acknowledge she'd been in the center of the spider's web, but the monster hadn't woken up. So, when she saw the back door was cracked open slightly, her heart jumped.

"Gary," she mumbled.

Did he actually sneak in there? That would have been completely out of character. He was a by-the-books kind of cop. He must have had a really good reason to stray from the straight and narrow path. That meant Maggie did too. As if she were walking a tightrope, she pushed the door in and stepped inside. It smelled funny.

With her breath hitched in her throat and every muscle tensed, Maggie stood just inside the threshold and listened. There was no sound. None at all. It was pitch dark. Her eyes wouldn't focus no matter how hard she stretched them open or squinted. Where was Gary? Maybe he wasn't even in the house. Maybe he hadn't noticed the door was cracked and had already slipped around the other side of the house and was on his way back to the car. He'd see she wasn't there and panic.

*What have you done? You've caused a ripple effect that's going to cost you. Margaret, do you ever use the brain God gave you?* Her conscience ripped at her. But before she could turn tail and dash out the door, there was a noise from the front of the house. A creak in a floorboard. Someone was in the house with her. But who was it? Should she call out? Should she turn and leave, hurrying back to the car like all she'd been doing was taking an evening stroll? Her mouth was dry, but beneath her arms she felt cold sweat. There was nothing she could do that wasn't going to be a bad decision at this point.

"Gary?" she whispered into the darkness.

"Maggie! I thought I told you to stay in the car!" Gary hissed.

Maggie clutched her stomach and let out the breath she'd been holding as she reached for her friend. She could tell when she placed her arm on his biceps that he was tense with anger. Quickly, she let go.

"I'm sorry. I know you did. But I remembered something about that night I was here, and it's important," she blathered. Had there been any light, Gary would have seen her tugging at her sleeves, wrinkling her nose, and squinting up at him.

"Come on. We have to get out of here before—"

At that precise moment, the sound of the electric garage door opener echoed through the house. Without warning, Gary reached out, grabbed Maggie, spun her around, and gave her a shove out the back door. The air was cooler outside. Or maybe it was that the fear wasn't as intense in the yard as it was inside, where neither one of them belonged. If she really thought about it, Maggie decided that all three of them were trespassing. Colleen too. Maybe especially.

In the soft light from the neighbor's back porch, Maggie turned and saw Gary put his index finger to his lips. She nodded. He took her hand. It was as natural a gesture as brushing a stray strand of hair from her forehead or smoothing out her collar. His hand was thick and solid, and she held it tightly.

Quickly and quietly, they slipped behind

another lilac bush on the other side of the house. The neighbors must have had a professional landscaper. There were tall trees and thick bushes separating the properties. On the one hand it provided extra shadows for Maggie and Gary to hide in. But it also was a safe haven for mosquitos and lightning bugs galore. Maggie took a swipe at a few buzzing things as she was led into the darkness. Gary pushed her against the siding of the house while he peeked over to see if anyone appeared behind them. The beam of a flashlight cut through the darkness from inside the house.

At first Maggie thought maybe the police had been called by a concerned neighbor who saw a couple of yahoos prowling around the house. But then she realized that it had to be Colleen. She had the code for the garage. How did she manage to get that?

She was about to pose the question to Gary when the light became brighter, and someone had stepped outside. Their shadowy silhouette shifted from one foot to the other. Instinctively, Maggie pressed her body harder against the siding and held her breath. Gary tensed. She was sure he was holding his breath too. After what felt like an hour, the beam of light swung around and disappeared.

Only the sound of the door closing, complete with the snap of a lock, was heard next. Both Maggie and Gary let their breaths out at the same time.

Again, he took her hand and pulled her into the neighbor's yard into the foliage and shadows. Maggie was surprised at how stealthily he moved. For such a big guy he had the grace of a gazelle. She, on the other hand, tripped over her own foot, bit her tongue when she regained her balance, and freaked out with arms flailing when she felt the tickle of a spiderweb across her cheek. But through it all she managed to remain quiet.

Once on the sidewalk away from Colleen's house, or more accurately, the house Colleen was squatting in, Gary squeezed Maggie's hand and pulled at her like a father scolding a child who had almost run into traffic.

"Margaret Bell! What were you thinking?"

"Gary, before you get mad at me, I had to tell you something. It couldn't wait."

"Yes. It could have. Do you know how much trouble you could have gotten us into?"

"Me? You're the one who was inside the house… without a warrant, might I add," she huffed as he pulled the passenger-side door open.

She climbed in, and he stood there with his

body between Maggie and the door. He leaned in as if he were talking to a suspect in a petty crime.

"Okay. You want to tell me what was so important that you had to disobey my order to stay put?" He had one arm draped over the top of the door, the other on his hip as he leaned in.

Maggie took a deep breath and explained what she had seen in Colleen's car. Then, she snapped her fingers and said she'd overheard Roger Hawes telling Sam at the thrift store that Colleen had lost his hammer.

"It's not a lock, but I'd bet good money that that hammer has Matthew's blood on it," Maggie said. "Plus, if she saw you, even if she knew you were a cop, I don't think she would hesitate to do something drastic and claim ignorance. She'd say she didn't know you were a cop, or she thought you were a burglar, or whatever might pop into her deranged mind," Maggie said, putting her hands up and wiggling her fingers at the word *deranged*.

Gary shook his head, looked at Maggie, and smirked.

"What?"

"I'm taking you home" was all he said before leaning back and shutting the door. Once he climbed behind the wheel and they were driving, Maggie couldn't be quiet.

"Did I do something wrong?"

"Where do you want me to start, Mags?" Gary chuckled.

"I'm being serious."

Gary looked at his watch and then to the left out the window as they drove. He didn't seem to be in any hurry.

"No. Well, yes. But no."

"What the heck does that mean?"

Officer Brookes took a deep breath before speaking. "First, you really could have gotten us pinched by not staying in the car. But"—he rolled his eyes—"I can see why you thought it was impor-tant to tell me what you knew."

"Do you think it will help with the case?"

"I can't say for sure. I've got to get the hammer first."

They sat in silence for a few moments until Maggie jumped in her seat, snapped her fingers, and shouted *"I know!"* making Gary almost lose control of the squad car.

"What do you know?"

"Tomorrow, I'll tell Colleen someone broke my window. She'll drive over. You can be waiting in the bushes and go check her car while I have her come in for some tea," Maggie said, finishing with a crazed smile and her eyebrows up.

"No. Being anywhere near that woman is too dangerous. Remember, she's hurt people. This isn't someone who just bounced a couple of checks," Gary insisted. "In fact, I don't even think you should go home tonight. I think you should stay somewhere else. Do you have a friend you can call?"

"Have we met?" Maggie asked sarcastically with her face twisted into a sneer. Of course she didn't have anyone to call to stay with. "Would you look what happened when I tried to make a new friend? She wants to kill me."

Gary couldn't help but chuckle. That made Maggie chuckle. "That's true."

They sat in comfortable silence again as Gary weaved his way down the quiet streets in the direction of Maggie's home. When he pulled up in the driveway, he told her to stay put again.

"I mean it. I'm just going to walk around your house and make sure everything looks okay. You stay right where you are." He pointed at her, his sculpted biceps bulging underneath his shirt. The look in his eyes made Maggie feel safe and a little jittery at the same time. Where did that feeling come from? She'd known Gary forever. There was no reason to be jittery around him. She blinked back but said nothing and nodded.

Gary pulled out his flashlight and shined it at her cottage. He walked around it, shined the light in the windows, and even inspected the roof and the trees around it. The damage to her window hadn't changed. Nothing more had been done to the property. For that Maggie was relieved. But as she watched the beam of light bounce along as Gary checked every window and behind every bush, she felt that spark in her gut. It was an unfamiliar feeling, but she knew what it was. It wasn't just annoyance like she felt at the bookstore when teenagers came in and whined about having to read *To Kill a Mockingbird* or *Romeo and Juliet*. It wasn't that awkwardness that came from horrific bouts of small talk with strangers. This was anger. Pure and simple. Maggie was angry. No. She was enraged. Someone had intentionally damaged her house. It wasn't an accident. It wasn't a random act of vandalism that caught her and a couple of neighbors with some petty repairs. It was intentional. Colleen Hawes had damaged her house and threatened her. *Intentionally.* And for what? That's what made no sense.

*I'm not that big. I'm not skilled at fighting. But I'm not going to take this kind of abuse from anyone.* Her little voice had suddenly grown very big. Maggie was through playing nice. She was going to catch Colleen and then throw the book at her.

## Chapter 21

After Gary left, Maggie's brave thoughts began to wane. It was a listless night. Every noise made Maggie's eyes pop wide open and her heart bang in her chest. She held her breath so many times straining to hear a strange noise or the sound of breaking glass that she was sure she could have caused herself to hyperventilate. When the sky started to lighten, she managed to squeeze in an hour of solid sack time. Getting out of bed to get ready for work was surprisingly easy.

Making it to work fifteen minutes early allowed Maggie some time to enjoy the smell of the cinnamon rolls Babs was baking, as well as get a small cup of coffee she could nurse in a quiet spot of the store, out of view of anyone peeking in the windows while waiting for the store to open.

"Maggie, the display is driving people wild," Babs said before Maggie retreated to the bookshop side of the café. "You have such a gift. I swear if it weren't for those you wouldn't have half the foot traffic you do. And that spillover for me too." She winked. Her long eyelashes waved like flags at the top of a sailboat.

"Thanks, Babs," Maggie said. She sat in her highbacked side chair, sipping her coffee and peeking at the display window. It did turn out pretty, but it was not the most important thing on her mind at the moment. Over and over, she turned the facts of her situation with Colleen in her brain. Finally, it was time to open the store.

Customers trickled in, and at first Maggie was pleasantly surprised at the lack of chitchat coming her way as well as how fast the time flew by. That is until a familiar face showed up that caused her blood to boil.

"Where's Joshua?" Roger Hawes barked.

Maggie wanted to ask him where his crazy niece was but held back. Instead, she just looked up at him and shrugged her shoulders. He was in his usual attire, except this morning his temples were sweaty, and he looked like he hadn't slept.

"How can you not know? He's the boss, ain't he?"

"Sometimes he has errands to run before he gets in. Maybe today is one of those days," she snapped back, wrinkling her nose and fidgeting nervously with the buttons of her cardigan. Even in the warmer months, she wore a sweater in the store. The air conditioning was in mint condition and brought a little bit of the arctic tundra to the bookstore.

"You tell him I need to talk to him as soon as he gets in. You got that?" Roger looked around as if he thought Maggie might be hiding Joshua behind the romance section or maybe in the window display.

Maggie nodded her head.

"Well, ain't you gonna write it down?"

"Believe me. I'll remember to tell him," Maggie replied.

Roger let out a short breath then gave a quick nod before he exited the bookstore. He took with him a nervous vibe that was palpable. Maggie watched him hustle past the display window without so much as a sideways glance, his head down and his steps clomping on the sidewalk.

"What's his problem?" Babs asked, startling Maggie out of her thoughts. She was standing at the register with a cinnamon roll the size of a quarter pounder.

"I'm not sure," Maggie replied.

"Well, he was loud enough to shake the windows in the café. Next time he comes in I'll have to explain to him how we use our indoor voice." She smirked. "Here. You are getting too thin. Have something sweet."

She handed the sweet roll to Maggie, who smiled.

"These smell wonderful," Maggie said as she took the small plate and fork.

"Wait until you taste it. It's my own recipe. I'm going to give the lady down the street a little healthy competition. You enjoy," she said before turning and strutting back to the café side of the store. She had her bleach-blond hair in a high ponytail with a red bandana around it, and her tight jeans were cuffed high over her ankles. Maggie wished she had Babs's confidence, especially at a time like this when the neighborhood bully made an appearance. But she didn't. She had Maggie Bell's confidence, and it was sorely lacking at times. But what she lacked in boldness she made up for in cunning. As she dug into her cinnamon roll and took the first bite, she wondered if Joshua was all right.

Could Roger have come in looking for him because he thought something bad had happened to him at the hands of his crazy niece? She mused as she ate, looking out the window to the street traffic.

"Maybe. Oh my gosh, this is delicious." Maggie rolled her eyes. As she slowly savored every bite of cinnamon roll that practically melted in her mouth, the lightest wafers of dough combined with the perfect amount of icing, she began to worry. Joshua hadn't mentioned being in late today. But he had been a little distracted lately and could have had some vendors to meet with or maybe even someone at the bank. Heck, he could have gone to cash in some pennies, and those hens would keep him there as long as possible if they thought they might capture his attention.

Maggie patted her belly when she returned the plate to Babs, who smiled wide. Her bright-red lipstick made her teeth look blindingly white.

"Glad you liked it," she said as she served up one to an older man in jeans, a dark blue baseball hat, and a plaid shirt, who appeared to be in no hurry to get to a job or any kind of appointment.

When he turned around with his roll and cup of coffee, the front of his cap had a single word in yellow letters. Retired.

"Babs, did Joshua tell you if he was going to be late today?" Maggie asked.

"If I remember right, he did say he had an appointment this week with the landlord of the building next door. I can't remember if it was today or not. But I know he was going to be late getting in sometime this week. Don't let that old blowhard worry you. That guy is all bark and no bite," Babs said while shaking her head.

At that moment the bells over the door jingled, and a book club of older ladies came shuffling in, chatting happily like a flock of sparrows. Maggie went back to the bookstore side feeling slightly better. But now she had a full belly, and the lack of sleep from the night before was starting to catch up to her. Once she started yawning, she couldn't stop.

Unlike the morning, the rest of the day dragged along. People came bustling in and out, but it seemed to Maggie like they stopped the clock instead of making it move faster. Still, there was no sign of Joshua. He hadn't come in or called, and that wasn't like him. Maggie looked at the calendar in the office, but there was nothing scribbled on today's date. Or any other date for that matter. None of them had an efficient scheduling method in place. That was something Maggie decided she was going to suggest to Joshua when she saw him again.

*If you see him again,* that little voice in her head scoffed. She shook the thought away, her dark curls bouncing around her face. She twisted her lip as she looked out the window.

*Of course you'll see him again. He's just out running errands. He's done it before. A million times. This is nothing new. You're just hypersensitive to the clock because of what happened last night,* she soothed herself. *Plus, you are painfully exhausted. You aren't even thinking straight because of your window and being out with Gary half the night.*

That had to be it. She was overtired. Every little thing was going to set her off because no matter how hard she tried, she wasn't thinking straight. With each passing moment her body became limper and limper. Each muscle ached as she helped customers with their requests. It felt like everyone wanted a book from a top shelf today, and that required Maggie to climb the ladder to reach them. She yawned a dozen times and had a second coffee in the late afternoon.

Finally, it was almost quitting time. Since Joshua

hadn't shown up all day or called, Maggie didn't see the harm in locking the place up fifteen minutes early. Babs didn't mind and had the café cleaned and ready for the next day in record time.

"I'll see you tomorrow, honey. Get some rest. You look beat," she said as she waved, left through the café door, and locked it up tight behind her.

Maggie was happy to be alone in the quiet bookstore. Although she was not worried about getting in trouble, she did decide to wait and see if Joshua showed up before shutting off the lights and counting out the register. She went to the office to get the bank bag, but before she was able to grab the bag, there was a knock on the glass. Her whole body slumped as she turned around, expecting to see someone looking at their watch with a grumpy face. How dare the bookstore be closed fifteen minutes early? They need to waste fifteen minutes. Where are they supposed to do it if Maggie locks it before closing time?

But it wasn't just some random customer. It wasn't someone looking to kill time. It was Colleen. Something told Maggie it wasn't a coincidence she was there.

# Chapter 22

As she tried to look casual sauntering to the door, Maggie gave a twisted, awkward smile, pointed to her watch, and mouthed the words "Closing time."

"Oh, come on, Maggie. You can let me in for just a second." Colleen smiled sweetly.

Maggie shook her head and raised her hands, palms up as she shrugged her shoulders.

"Well, if you don't let me in, you won't ever know what happened to your boss," Colleen replied as if she was just telling Maggie the forecast called for rain later in the evening.

Suddenly her limbs became like lead. Lead that had been stowed in a meat locker for a solid sixty minutes or so. It was the coldness in Colleen's eyes that froze her down to the marrow in her bones. Maggie tilted her head to the left and rolled her eyes as if to convey her confusion, as fake as it was. She knew exactly what Colleen was saying, and it made her annoyed and angry that she would play such a stupid game at this point.

So, without any further hesitation, she walked up to the door, snapped the dead bolt back, and pulled open the door. The bells jingled loudly, echoing through the bookstore as loud as a gong. Maggie stepped back and let Colleen enter.

"That's better. At least I asked permission, unlike you did last night when you and that big ox were traipsing through my house. But that will be taken care of later. Officer Brookes, that's his name, right? Yeah, well, he'll have some explaining to do before he's forced to resign," Colleen said. She was wearing tight blue jeans and a plain T-shirt as if she might be on her way to work on a house for flipping or planting a big garden.

"You were going to do the same thing at my house during Mrs. Peacock's party. But I was home. In *my* home where I pay rent. The real owners of that house you are squatting in are in Florida. How did you even get in there?" Maggie asked. She didn't really care how Colleen got into that house.

She did feel a tug of concern for the family that owned the house. But her inquiry was nothing more than a delay tactic. Maggie had to figure out how to get away. She should have never opened the door.

"Yeah, I guess that's true. But unlike you, as far as anyone knows I haven't killed anyone. You, on the other hand, killed Matthew Spencersmith because he turned down your advances," Colleen said with such confidence that her expression made Maggie gasp.

"I didn't kill anyone. You know I didn't." Maggie squinted with her eyebrows pinched in the middle. "As for advances on anyone, ha! I keep to myself, and everyone knows that."

Colleen chuckled. "Sure you do. Everyone knows it's the quiet ones who are the most danger-ous. You killed Spencersmith with a hammer. You wanted him to use his budding political connections to help Joshua Whitfield cut through the red tape around this building and his claim to it. In exchange you offered him a romantic encounter. But he knocked you back because he loves his fiancée. You didn't like that one bit, did you? And all that pent-up rage just couldn't be contained. So, in your head it was hammer time." Colleen chuckled as Maggie felt her stomach fold over on itself.

"That's as convoluted a plan as the hostage rescue attempt during the Carter administration." Maggie blurted out the words. When she saw Colleen's neck flush bright red with fury, she wished she could take them back.

"My uncle is going to get this property. Your desperate measures didn't stop with Spencersmith, and poor, poor Joshua Whitfield will be your final victim. Mona Plum will testify to your temper. She's got the proof of it all over her face." Colleen smirked.

Roger Hawes has been after this property for years, but Maggie never dreamed he'd kill for it. Worse, have his psychotic niece do the dirty work for him.

"You really are out of your mind," Maggie muttered. "So is your uncle."

"Don't you say a word about him!" Colleen shouted as she reached into her big purse. Maggie froze as she waited to see the horrible image of a gun or worse. Instead it was the hammer she had seen in the back of Colleen's car. The murder weapon used to kill Matthew Spencersmith.

Maggie tried to think how to defend herself. She wasn't strong, so hand-to-hand combat was out of the question. She didn't have a weapon of any kind and was surrounded by nothing but books, and most of those were soft cover. That did it. Her best option was flight. Dash for the front door that pulls into the store or make a wild run to the storeroom where the door pushes open out to the alley?

*Push,* Maggie thought.

"My uncle has been more than reasonable and patient. He's been like a father to me. There isn't anything I wouldn't do for him," Colleen said as she swung the hammer.

"Obviously," Maggie muttered, unable to control her sarcasm. *You aren't helping yourself,* her thoughts scolded. But still, she ran her mouth. "Mona knew you were sick, didn't she? That's why she didn't want anything to do with you. It had nothing to do with the fairy story you told me. She was on to you, and you thought—"

"I thought I could take her, but she had a little more gas in the tank than I expected. Turned out okay, though. She thinks it was you who tried to kill her. We aren't much different in size, and a hoody with a mask makes everyone look the same. Still a win-win for my team." Colleen took a step forward as Maggie inched back.

"What did I ever do to you? I didn't even know

you until a couple days of ago. I thought we were friends." Maggie huffed.

"I don't need friends. What I need is for you to shut up and go to the back of the store," Colleen hissed. Time was up. There was no more stalling. Maggie had no choice but to do as she was told and focus on a plan to get out of this jam with her head still attached to her body.

"What are you planning on doing?" Maggie asked just above a whisper.

"I'm going to kill you. But not until after I've killed your boss to make it look like you did it. I was able to practice a little bit with Matthew. I see where I screwed up. I had hoped with the body on your property and your prints on the weapon they'd scoop you up lickety-split. But I was off on my calculations." Colleen seemed happy to explain her plan. Maggie had been sure she'd get a "shut up" or "keep quiet" but no. It was a free exchange of information.

"How?"

Colleen stepped toward Maggie and forced her to walk backward into the small cubby that was the office. Without even being aware of it, Maggie raised her hands in the surrender pose. "Oh, that big dummy of a cop. He's not as stupid as he looks.

I didn't realize you guys were friends or that you were sweet on him."

"What? Sweet on him? What are you talking about? No one is sweet on anybody. I just know him from town. We went to high school together. Sweet on him? Are you crazy? Well… yes, I suppose you are. But I'm not sweet on anyone." Maggie lied for fear that if Colleen knew any more about her relationship with Gary that he'd be in mortal danger too. "He's just the local constable. A beat cop. Nothing more. That's it."

Colleen smirked. "So you're sweet on him. Hmm. Maybe I picked the wrong victim. Oh well. Too late to change the plan now." Without warning, Colleen hauled back her fist then let it fly, all the while with a smile on her face. The last thing Maggie remembered was a punch in the face. Then black.

When she came to, Maggie had no idea what time it was. Her head pounded, and in short order she realized she was on the floor with her hands tied behind her back. There was a scarf or rag in her mouth. For an instant her stomach jumped at the thought of one of the cleaning rags from the bathroom closet in her maw. But there was no chemical taste or smell.

*She must have brought her own gag,* Maggie thought. It felt like a hot ball of lead was rolling around in her head. Part of her wanted to just go limp again on the floor, close her eyes, and let whatever happened next just happen without her. But there was that other part of her that had been getting increasingly bolder. The part that prompted her to spy on people, to trespass on private property, to make sarcastic remarks out loud without mumbling. That budding new blossom was pushing her to act.

Thankfully, the gag around her mouth was just that, and there was no threat of choking. But the huge strip of duct tape over the gag and part of her nose was causing a big problem. Each breath she took was shallow and hot. Only her own carbon dioxide was being inhaled. Her hands were bound tightly behind her with more duct tape. Her legs were bound at the ankles. She tugged and twisted but couldn't get enough slack to pull her wrists through. Looking down she saw the duct tape digging into her skin. All the adrenaline racing through her body kept the pain at bay. But it wouldn't be long before she started to lose the sensation in her feet.

It was then that Maggie heard someone knocking on the front door. Colleen's footsteps clomped across the hardwood floor of the store in that direction away from the office.

"Hello?" Colleen called politely.

*Oh gosh. Who is it? Who is there? She's liable to go nuts on them.* Maggie's thoughts raced. Out of a dark corner appeared Poe, who came quickly up to Maggie's side, purring and butting his head against hers.

"Uh, hello?" Joshua asked more than stated.

*No! Joshua's here. What is she going to do to him? She's going to punch him or use her hammer that she never returned to her uncle. What in the world am I going to do?* Maggie looked at Poe, who purred right into her face before leaping silently onto the desk and perching himself there, proudly unaware and uninterested in her dilemma. For a split second Maggie wished she was the silky black cat without a care in the world and nothing better to do but find a square of sunshine on the window sill and lay in it.

"Hi. You must be Joshua," Colleen purred as she introduced herself. "I'm Maggie's friend. I've heard so much about you. Her description of you was spot-on."

*What? I didn't describe anything. You have not heard so much about him! I never said practically anything about Joshua! How dare you!* Maggie gritted her teeth.

"Um, where is she? I need to talk to her. You do know the store is closed now?" Joshua said. Was he rebuking her flirty behavior? Of course he was. He wasn't dumb enough to fall for that babe-in-the-woods act.

"She said she had to do something out in the alley really quickly and would be right back," Colleen replied. "I've been dying to ask you how you got into this business. Have you always liked books? I enjoy reading myself."

*What a load of manure. She is sweet-talking him just like she did to me.* Maggie raged inside. Perhaps it was petty. At this inopportune moment Maggie was experiencing a bout of extreme jealousy. With her hands and feet bound, a gag in her mouth, and a right eye that was becoming harder and harder to see out of from the punch in the face, she did know this was not the time for jealousy. But she didn't care. Of course she understood Joshua's life was in danger. But she couldn't help the territorial feeling that swept over her. It wasn't that she thought of Joshua as hers. She didn't. She keenly aware that he wasn't hers. But that didn't mean she was about to let some bargain-basement fatal-attraction type sweet-talk him so she could kill him.

*And then blame you when you are crazy about him,* her inner voice whined.

*Okay, maybe not crazy. But severely fond of him. Is that better?*

*Why are you arguing with yourself over this now? Get ahold of yourself, Mags! She's going to kill him and then you if you don't pull your head out of the clouds!*

With all her strength Maggie tried to pull out of her restraints. Colleen must have done this before because the duct tape was impossible to budge.

"Uh, yeah. What did Maggie say she was doing in the alley? She's got the place locked up and—"

"Yeah. Well, we were going out tonight for a couple of drinks. She told me to meet her here after work, and we were going to go paint the town red. She told me what happened at her house. I thought she could use a little cheering up," Colleen purred.

"What happened at her house?"

Maggie immediately picked up on the concern in Joshua's voice. With renewed vigor she struggled to get free. Her sudden movement startled Poe, who jumped down from the desk, knocking a pair of scissors onto the faux-Persian rug that was underneath it. Maggie's eyes bugged out of her skull. Like a worm that finds itself on the sidewalk, she wriggled over to it. Clumsily, she managed to get her the scissors awkwardly in her hands. The hard part was figuring out how to cut her hands loose. Every way she manipulated the scissors wasn't good enough. She just couldn't make it work. Every book she'd ever read with a hero being bound and gagged flashed through her mind, each one making her madder and madder by the second because she knew she wasn't going to fall into a river and float off to safety or have a wise-cracking sidekick show up to cut her loose. Nope. She had a pair of scissors in her hand, and Crazy Colleen was going to kill Joshua and then her. End of story. To add insult to injury, she could clearly hear Colleen talking.

"Oh, she didn't tell you? Last night someone threw a rock and a book through her window. It really freaked her out. I would have thought she called you right away. The way she talks about you, I just thought…"

Maggie's hands were slick with sweat. How did Colleen know what happened last night? Maggie hadn't told a soul, and she knew darn well that Gary didn't speak of it in mixed company. The only way Colleen could know is if she did it. Maggie rolled her eyes. Of course she knew Colleen had done it.

"What? Is she okay?"

*Yes! Yes! I'm okay! Actually, I've been better!* Maggie screamed in her head.

"Yeah. She's fine. You should probably go out into the alley to talk to her. You'll see. She's fine," Colleen said.

"I'll just wait for her to get back in," Joshua replied.

Maggie looked around. What could she do? What could she bump into to get someone's attention? If only she could kick over the umbrella stand or the coatrack or...

Finally, a spark of an idea came to her. She couldn't get the scissors to cooperate cutting the binds around her wrists. But she could cut her legs free. With the scissors in a death grip, Maggie was able to open them up. While laying on her side, she bent her knees, pulling her legs behind her so her ankles almost touched her bottom. She held her breath as she slipped the blade beneath the tape. She could hear the conversation in the other part of the store.

"Uh... that's fine. Tell me, where are you and Maggie planning on going tonight?" Joshua asked pleasantly.

*Nowhere! We weren't going anywhere! I don't drink, Joshua! You know that! You of all people know that!*

Maggie screamed on the inside. Her breath was coming in short bursts. The moisture of each pant was loosening the duct tape but not nearly fast enough for her to shout out to Joshua. With each clumsy jerk of the scissors, she could feel the tape starting to give. She could also feel the pointed end poking into her ankle. The pain was there, but Maggie found it easy to ignore.

"We were going to go to that place over on the north side of town. I can't remember the name. Maggie said she knew how to get there," Colleen said.

"That sounds like fun," Joshua replied, not only intensifying Maggie's terror and anxiousness but adding annoyance into the mix. Didn't he know her at all? Hadn't any of their encounters together meant anything to him? Oh, why did she even waste a thought on him when there was a perfectly good guy on the police force who knew her better than anyone else?

"Yes. Uh, maybe you should go see what's keeping her. I don't think whatever she had to do would take this long," Colleen insisted.

Maggie panicked and feverishly pushed the open blade of the scissors into the duct tape. Thank goodness they were a sharp pair.

"You're right. Uh, ladies first," Joshua said and extended his arm for Colleen to go ahead of him.

"Oh, uh, whoever heard of a lady going first into an alley." She chuckled nervously. "What if there is a mugger or a slasher or a vampire back there? You'd better go first."

There was a hesitation, but within a few seconds Joshua was walking toward the back door. Maggie was in the dark in the office cubby. There was just the light from the store illuminating the things around her. Joshua would walk past without even seeing her, and that is exactly what he did. Colleen was on his heels, the hammer raised, when suddenly from out of nowhere, a black form, long and lanky, jumped from a tall bookcase. A hiss and a yelp from Colleen meant Maggie knew exactly what had happened. Those extra seconds that Poe bought her were just enough for her to break the tape around her ankles and scramble to her feet. She staggered out of the dark cubby like a wino from an alley. Her eyes were wide, her words muffled, but Poe had pounced on Colleen with such force Joshua stopped, whirled around, and was staring at the whole spectacle. Funny. Maggie remembered Poe had always hissed when Colleen had come into the store.

"Maggie!" he gasped.

Maggie screamed behind the tape, but it only came out as a muffled grunt. Colleen kicked at Poe, making the cat hiss again and dart away to the safety of the shadows beneath Maggie's favorite sitting chair.

All this time Maggie thought she was the weaker opponent. Her entire life she considered herself nothing more than an awkward wallflower who had a big cop friend to hide behind if need be. But at this moment her true potential revealed itself. Colleen realized she might have gone a step too far. Kicking Poe sent Maggie into a rage. With her arms still bound behind her and her mouth taped shut, she narrowed her eyes, dropped her chin, and barreled into Colleen. She rammed her head into Colleen's gut, forcing out a painful and unladylike grunt before knocking her to the ground. Then there was a loud thud and the clamor of the hammer as it clattered across the floor out of Colleen's reach. Maggie was sure the thud was Colleen's head hitting the hardwood floor. But the force of her charge was so great Maggie toppled over too. Thankfully, Colleen broke most of her fall. After a second, Maggie collected her thoughts but still had no idea what she should do next. She was sure she jumped up like a prize fighter at the count of eight, but in reality, it might have been more like a drunken sailor climbing up onto a barstool.

"Oh! My head! You're crazy!" Colleen croaked and coughed.

"Mo! Mats to!" Maggie's cry was garbled beneath the tape as she backed away.

Joshua rushed up to her and clumsily fumbled with the restraints. Desperate to be free she tugged and pulled and finally got one hand out from the tape then ferociously ripped it from her mouth. It stung badly, making her gasp. But that didn't stop her from running her mouth.

"No! That's you! You're the crazy one! You killed Matthew Spencersmith, and you attacked Mona Plum! You did it! She did it, Joshua, and she was going to kill you, too, and pin it on me!" Maggie's chest heaved as she gulped air.

"That's just not true," Colleen replied with tears in her eyes as she started to get up.

"You better stay put! You think you can try and hurt my cat and I'm going to let you walk away? You are crazier than everyone says you are!" Maggie hissed as Joshua slipped his arm around her waist to hold her back.

"Joshua, I think Maggie's obsession with you

has made her an extremely jealous and dangerous person, and you might want to rethink her employment here at—" Colleen said before trying to get up.

"I'll show you dangerous!" Maggie shouted, windmilling her arms and kicking her feet in Colleen's direction, keeping the woman on the floor.

"Settle down, Mags. It's all right," Joshua said. "I know she's lying. I knew from the second I walked in here that something was wrong. You don't know Maggie very well. She doesn't drink. At all. Everyone knows that."

Maggie wanted nothing more than to look deeply into Joshua's eyes, smile, and kiss him full on the lips. Instead, she smirked at Colleen. It felt *almost* as good.

It was at that moment that a figure emerged from the back room. Maggie froze. All the fight drained out of her. She was no match for this person. He glared at Maggie then focused on Colleen before speaking.

"Get up" was all he said.

## Chapter 23

"**R**oger. You need to leave. This is a matter for the police, and you aren't going to take her anywhere. She's a danger to anyone around her, and that includes you." Joshua let go of Maggie and put his hands up in front of him.

Roger Hawes looked like he was about to cry. But the very idea of displaying such emotion, especially in the presence of two people he didn't like, was out of the question. He would choke down his emotions and let them fester in his gut like they always had.

"Uncle Roger." Colleen suddenly shifted her attitude and scrambled to her feet while holding her gut. "Thank goodness you showed up. They were about to kill me," she said as she put her other hand to the back of her head.

"They?" Joshua barked.

"I came to talk to them about the sale of the store, and they lost control. If you hadn't walked in, I don't know what would have happened to me." Colleen choked on her words and dabbed the corner of her eye with her index finger.

"Are you really believing this line of garbage?" Maggie's voice cracked. Joshua squeezed her around the waist as if to say keep quiet. She pinched her lips together and wrinkled her nose. Reluctantly she relaxed.

"I know what you've done, Colleen. Don't try and blame these people." Roger's voice was deep and gravelly.

"What I've done? Uncle Roger, I don't know what you're talking about." Colleen looked nervously at him, to Maggie, then back to her uncle. "You don't have to worry. Now that they've showed their hand that they'd kill anyone who tried to take their store and disrupt their little lives, you'll be able to buy this place lock, stock, and barrel."

"What?" Joshua squeezed Maggie tighter without realizing it. Maggie could feel the anger there and gently put her hand on his arm at her waist.

"I told you to stay out of it. Now, Colleen, I have an important question to ask you. Where is Ms. Feedle?" Roger asked.

"Oh, that busybody. She left. She went on vacation or something. I'm not sure." Colleen shrugged and looked down at the floor and at her nails and then out the front windows. Maggie tensed, as there was obviously some weight to this question, but she didn't know how much. Who was Ms. Feedle, and why would Colleen know where she was?

"Don't lie to me, Colleen. Just don't start this way. She hasn't been seen since you arrived in town. You are living in one of the houses she was showing. Where is she?" Roger asked.

But Colleen just stood there defiantly. She didn't say anything and glared at her uncle. It was obvious there had been another murder committed. All the fight drained out of Maggie, and she pressed her back against Joshua's chest for support. Suddenly, the reality of the situation hit her. It could have so easily been her. She was in that house alone. No one knew where she was. Her mouth went dry, and a shiver shook her body.

It was then that Gary walked in from the alley.

He also looked like a man who'd found a scratch on his brand-new pickup truck. He'd told Maggie that he was aware of more that was going on than she knew about. It would have been easy to get annoyed with him for not sharing that he was on to Colleen's shenanigans, but right now he was her real knight in shining armor.

"Colleen, what have you done? You can't stand there and look at me like that. I might be the only friend you have right now. Please," Roger pleaded.

"You mean *I* might be the only friend *you've* got. You've burnt every bridge in this lousy town. You wanted this building, and I was just minutes away from securing that for you. This is how you repay me? Nice, Uncle Roger. Real nice," Colleen hissed as she rubbed her stomach.

Maggie and Joshua stood stone-still. Gary walked around Roger, pulled his handcuffs from his utility belt, and softly started to read Colleen her Miranda rights.

"I didn't do anything wrong!" Colleen screamed. "Uncle Roger! Tell them it was her!"

When Roger didn't make a move to help or even part his lips to speak, Colleen went into a full-blown temper tantrum. It was so bad Maggie saw Gary reach for his pepper spray. She and Joshua instinctively backed up, and so did Roger. When Colleen realized that she'd either get ahold of herself or get doused in pepper spray, she bit her lip, raised her chin, and let Gary lead her out of the bookstore through the storeroom and alley. Roger looked at Joshua but said nothing before turning and following his niece.

Maggie pulled the last of the tape from her wrists. She was exhausted and exhilarated all at the same time. Joshua took a step back, folded his arms, and smirked as he looked Maggie up and down.

"What are you looking at?" she asked with her face in a sour pinch.

"I just witnessed Maggie Bell in a fight. I just can't believe it," he replied.

"You saw what she did to Poe. He was your dad's cat. Anyone who will hurt a pet will hurt a person. Well, she did more than hurt a person. She killed a person. Actually, she killed more than one. Two. That we know of," Maggie babbled as the adrenaline found its way to her mouth and kept it running.

"I've got to tell you, Maggie, you are really full of surprises," Joshua said.

"Yeah. Well, don't you forget it," Maggie said in nervous response. She didn't know what to say.

Taking on Colleen was not what she had planned. Her plan was to push her out of the way to get Joshua's attention, then he could wrestle her to the ground or lock her in a closet or clunk her on the head. That's what guys do. They come to the rescue. They save the day.

"Let me ask you a question. There was this bully in my eighth-grade class who kept taking my lunch money. How about we go pay him a visit, and you get my lunch money back," Joshua teased.

"Very funny. I'm not a bodyguard," Maggie huffed.

"You could have fooled me," Joshua continued. Maggie was sure he was enjoying making her blush. The smile on his face and the twinkle in his eyes infuriated her as they also totally disarmed her. The sarcasm she spoke so fluently hitched in the back of her throat. All she could do was turn red.

"I think I better get to the police station. They're going to have to take a statement. I wish the holding cell was in another room. That woman scared me," Maggie confessed.

"You proved you could take her." Joshua smiled.

"I proved I could let my temper get the best of me. It's a miracle from heaven that she didn't get a second wind. I hate to think of what she could have done."

"Maggie, *you* put her down. I think that's what happens when someone like you is finally able to do and be exactly what they were made for. You aren't just some wallflower," Joshua said. His choice of words made Maggie take a deep breath. She'd always referred to herself as a wallflower. She just did a few minutes ago. She was awkward and clumsy and nerdy and never fit in anywhere.

"You've got a spark. You should let it show more often."

Unable to control her smile, Maggie nodded. "Thanks, Joshua. I appreciate that."

"Just don't let it go to your head. You could take Colleen because she was a hot mess. Now me, on the other hand, I don't think you could take me."

"I could," Maggie said as she grabbed a light coat from the hook on the wall in the office cubby. It had been Alexander's. She'd worn it so many times during her employment at the shop it was almost a permanent fixture.

"No. You couldn't," Joshua insisted.

"What you don't know is I have been trained by the master," Maggie said with a completely straight face.

"The master?"

"Yes, Master M. A. Klutz."

"Did he teach you those windmill punches you were throwing?" Joshua laughed.

"Yes, he's the one." Maggie chuckled along with him. Even though they were headed to the police station and Maggie was apprehensive, it was something she had to do, and having Joshua there made it better. Easier. Maybe he was right. Maybe she wasn't supposed to be a wallflower. At least not all the time. Maybe she was supposed to stand out like her window displays did.

# Chapter 24

I t took a long time at the police station for Gary to take Maggie's statement because Colleen howled and shouted and interrupted and pleaded, only to start the whole thing all over again after a couple of minutes being quiet. By the time Maggie got out of there, it was almost daytime. As Joshua drove her home, he told her to take the day off, and she was happy to do so.

"Try not to get in any trouble from the driveway to your house," he teased as he pulled up the short gravel drive.

"If I wasn't so tired, I'd have a really snappy comeback and maybe a hand gesture to go with it. You're lucky, Whitfield." She yawned as she got out of the car and waved good-bye. As she looked at her cottage, she saw the window had been fixed. That was quick. She saw there was no notice of eviction stapled to the front door. That was also a plus.

For a brief second before she opened her front door, Maggie took a deep breath and looked around the yard. It really was a beautiful little piece of land. Mrs. Peacock had excellent taste. Of course, sitting on a small fortune helped. But if she did leave, it would be hard, if not impossible, to find a better view. Without thinking about it anymore, Maggie went inside, shut the door, and snapped the lock in place.

There was a brilliant sunset when Maggie's eyes popped open. Was someone actually knocking on the door?

"Maybe it's just exploding head syndrome," Maggie muttered. She'd heard about the phenomenon of people who are asleep and wake up hearing knocking on a door or breaking glass. They check everything out. No one knocking. No shards of glass on the ground. But the sound woke them up. It was referred to as exploding head syndrome. Just as she was about to go back to sleep, she heard the knock again.

"Well, my head isn't exploding," she grumbled

as she walked to the door. On tiptoes she squinted through the peephole and saw Mrs. Peacock. Her heart sank. This was it. She'd have thirty days to vacate the premises. After a deep breath and an internal pep talk, Maggie pulled the door open.

"Maggie, I heard about everything that happened. Are you all right? Is there anything I can do for you?" Mrs. Peacock gushed.

"You heard already?" Maggie rubbed her eyes and yawned. "Did I sleep a couple of days?" she muttered more to herself than Mrs. Peacock.

"Mrs. Donovan called and asked if it wasn't Margaret Bell who was my tenant, and I said yes, of course. She's been my tenant for years. If it wasn't for her, I would barely be able to make ends meet. Well, Mrs. Donovan went on to tell me what she'd heard over the police scanner last night and what was on the news this morning. That awful Colleen Hawes has completely lost her mind and confessed to everything, stating her only regret was underestimating her nemesis. Well, you can imagine my reaction when Mrs. Donovan told me and…"

Maggie didn't hear much of what else Mrs. Peacock said. She was too shocked to hear her actions had shocked someone else. She yawned again and refocused on Mrs. Peacock.

"That brings me to this." She handed a large envelope to Maggie.

"What is it?"

"It's my way of saying I'm sorry. I am responsible for this happening to you. I should have apologized sooner and offered for you to stay somewhere safer, somewhere out of the way, until things died down," she replied.

"If you'd have done that we might have never caught on to Colleen, and who knows what other bits of damage she'd have done." Maggie soothed her. She looked down at the envelope and flipped the metal brads that held it shut. What she pulled out was a deed.

"I've written you into my will. This cottage and one quarter of an acre around it is yours if you want it. I've owned this property free and clear for several years. You won't owe any kind of mortgage. Only the yearly property tax for your portion." Mrs. Peacock held her head up and looked down her nose at Maggie. "Good tenants are hard to find. I don't want to lose you."

Maggie looked behind her then scratched her head. "Am I still dreaming?"

"I don't think so," Mrs. Peacock replied before clearing her throat. "You can sign it and give it back to me in the morning. I'll have my lawyers tend to everything else."

"I don't know what to say, Mrs. Peacock. I'm… in shock." Maggie had read a million rags-to-riches stories over the course of her life. She had been so mad at Mrs. Peacock that she was sure her temper had gotten her a one-way ticket to Evictionville. Never in a million years would she have thought the old broad would have done something so wonderful. Even if all she'd said was *please don't leave*, Maggie would have been happy with that. Overjoyed even. She would have stayed and continued paying Mrs. Peacock the rent that kept her from the soup lines. But this was a gift she'd never expected.

She wasn't sure if it was because she was still tired or because she was overcome with emotions, but tears filled her eyes. She stepped out of the house and did something she'd never done before. She hugged Mrs. Peacock. Tight.

"You let me know if there is anything I can do for you. Now or in the future," Mrs. Peacock said as she hugged Maggie back.

"You are a real lady, Mrs. Peacock. I can't thank you enough."

Mrs. Peacock pulled back, cleared her throat, and lifted her chin. "I should have done this some time ago. Anyone who was thought of so highly by Alexander Whitfield I should have known was the kind of person I want around me. Good night, my dear." Mrs. Peacock smiled and turned, her elegant muumuu fluttering in the soft breeze, her kitten heels clicking along the sidewalk.

"Mrs. Peacock, I do have one favor to ask."

## Chapter 25

The music was lively, and the air smelled of charcoal on the grill. People were chatting and laughing as Maggie fluttered around in a pretty summer dress and flip-flops. She had never had anyone to her cottage before, let alone everyone she knew.

Babs and her husband Roy were on the front stoop. Their son, Earl, was sleeping, even with all the noise and a little breeze blowing. Gary, who was the first to arrive, was hunched over a tiny balcony barbeque pit grilling three burgers at a time while laughing with Casper and his girlfriend. Mrs. Peacock was sitting very matronly in a chaise lounge she'd had one of her landscapers pull across her yard to Maggie's. But it was Joshua who was entertaining everyone.

"You had to be there to believe it. Maggie? How much do you weigh?" Joshua called to her as she emerged from the cottage with a fresh pitcher of lemonade.

"Joshua Whitfield! You should know better than to ask a lady that question!" Mrs. Peacock scolded and smirked before she looked down to admire the jewelry on her fingers.

"Yeah. I weigh between *none of* and *your business*," Maggie replied, making Babs and Roy burst out laughing.

"Fine. Keep it to yourself. But you should have seen her. Colleen went to kick Poe and—"

"She tried to kick that sweet cat?" Casper's girlfriend joined the conversation. Maggie thought she was a pretty girl and seemed sweet. If she remembered, her name was Paulette or Pauline. It was hard to keep track. Casper, who was a quiet young man, must have had something all the girls wanted because he had a different sweetheart every six months. Maggie was sure it was because he was such a gentleman.

"Yes. But I'll bet that's the last time she ever

does that! Maggie was like a bull that saw red! She ducked down and charged with every bit of her weight behind her and knocked Colleen Hawes to the ground. She saved my life," Joshua bragged.

"Hey, Mags. You know the police department is hiring. You might want to consider working for the city. Sounds like you've got the stuff," Gary said as he came over carrying a platter of burgers. Maggie had a table set that she'd borrowed from Mrs. Peacock's patio. There were chips and potato salad and crudités along with a stack of paper plates and cups.

"I think you need to put one of those burgers in your mouth," Maggie teased. Although it was a terrible experience dealing with Colleen, Maggie had realized one very important thing. She was a lot more than she'd ever thought she was. She still wasn't sure what she was, but she wasn't a wallflower. That was a term she was never going to refer to herself as again.

"Don't tell her that. I need her at the bookstore," Joshua piped up.

"Does anyone know what happened to Roger Hawes?" Babs asked.

Roy shrugged. Joshua rolled his eyes. Gary took

a deep breath, but it was Mrs. Peacock who answered that question.

"His pawn shop is closed for the time being. I think he's considering selling and leaving Fair Haven. Colleen's reputation has made people wary of purchasing anything for fear that she might see it as an unfair acquisition and go after them."

Gary looked at Joshua. "You ought to buy his pawn shop, Josh. Wasn't he trying to get his hands on your place? That would be an ironic turn of events."

"You know, all of this was because he wanted my shop. I don't know why. There are buildings all over Main Street that are for rent or for sale. He could have gotten a better deal with any one of them. I don't know what it was about our place that had him so dead set on owning it." Joshua stood and began to help himself to the food. Maggie followed behind him.

"He was always after your dad. He was not a nice man," Maggie mumbled. She recalled his behavior at the funeral of Alexander Whitfield and how the property was the only thing he was concerned with. Who acts that way at a funeral?

*Someone who is crazy,* Maggie thought but didn't say.

"Well, it's all over now. Life can go back to normal here in Fair Haven," Casper added before giving his girl a sweet peck on the cheek.

Just then a black Lexus pulled up the tiny gravel driveway and parked. With the engine still running, the back driver's-side door opened, and a tall, elegant blond woman stepped out. Maggie recognized her instantly. She walked down her stoop and approached the woman.

"I didn't know you were having a party," Mona Plum said. She still had a bruise on her cheek. It had gone from a dark purple to a jaundiced yellow but would be gone in the next day or two.

"It's okay. Would you like to join us? It's just burgers and lemonade, but you are welcome to…" Maggie said.

Mona didn't smile or frown. She looked to all the guests, who were talking, and Maggie was sure she took a deep breath of the smokey barbeque.

"No. I've got another engagement, and then I'm leaving. I don't think I fit in around here," she said. Her snobby attitude clung to her like lint pearls on a sweater.

"Okay," Maggie replied. She didn't feel it was her place to make Mona feel comfortable. Maybe a week ago she might have tried to accommodate. But not today. This was her house and her party. If Mona didn't want to stay that was all right.

"I heard what happened. Colleen, she had quite a plan rolling around in her head along with her marbles. Trying to pin a murder on another person because she thought it would help her uncle get a piece of property?" Mona scoffed.

Maggie swallowed hard. She was waiting for some kind of peace offering. Maybe even an apology. But it was obvious the way she was looking at everything but Maggie that that was not going to happen.

"I knew she was dangerous. She gave off a really bad vibe."

"Were you ever friends with her?"

Mona went to speak but changed her mind. "Good luck to you, Maggie."

"You, too, Mona." Maggie extended her hand. Mona shook it limply before turning and getting back in the backseat of the car. She had a driver. Maggie wondered if it was a car service or her own personal chauffeur. The car pulled out of the driveway and sped away.

Maggie smoothed the front of her dress, turned, and went back to her guests.

"What did she want?" Mrs. Peacock asked.

"She heard about everything and just wanted to say good luck. Gary, you haven't eaten all the burgers, have you?" Maggie teased.

"Why would I do that? You might beat me up," he replied, making everyone laugh. The chatter continued. The music played. Everyone enjoyed themselves as the sun started to set.

## About the Author

Harper Lin is a 3x *USA TODAY* bestselling cozy mystery author. When she's not reading or writing mysteries, she loves going to yoga classes, hiking, and baking with her family and friends.

For a complete list of her books by series, visit her website.

www.HarperLin.com